# ULTIMATE
# RESOLUTION

TO VERNON;

BEST,

AZ

# *Al Dugan*

ISBN: 1547276509
ISBN-13: 9781547276509
Library of Congress Control Number: 2017911016
CreateSpace Independent Publishing Platform
North Charleston, South Carolina

Special thanks to Aaron Dugan Morrill for design of the cover.

# CHAPTER 1

## DOWN FOR THE COUNT

Alan awoke, able to open only his right eye. He had a bandage over his left eye and could feel the pull of stitches near his left eye. The light was blinding, and he felt extraordinary wracking pain over his entire body despite his high threshold for pain. The heart monitor was singing a rhythmic beeping, and several drip bags were hanging nearby.

Where am I?

All he remembered was the massive explosion, and it had all gone black. He had known it was a huge risk to set off all the charges early, but he had no other choice. If he hadn't set off all the charges early, he would have been dead. Everything had gone very wrong right at the end.

A beautiful nurse in starched whites entered the room and walked over to his bed. "Mr. Ramos, I am so glad to see you awake. How is the pain?" she asked with a big smile and a definite Colombian-Spanish accent.

"I am okay." Alan grimaced, answering in Spanish with his best Castilian accent. "Where am I?"

"You are in a private hospital in Cartagena. Two men brought you here. Do you remember the accident?"

A tumble of vivid images flooded Alan's mind.

The nurse checked his vital signs. She updated the chart and asked, "Anything I can get for you, Mr. Ramos?"

"No, thank you," Alan said before closing his eye. He heard the nurse leave and carefully checked under his pillow, looking for his Beretta. No Beretta. He was completely defenseless. He had no idea who the two men were who had brought him to the hospital.

Alan pressed the call button for the nurse, and she arrived in a few minutes. "How can I help you, Mr. Ramos?"

"I would like to make a telephone call. I don't see a telephone. Can you bring me one?"

"I am so sorry, Mr. Ramos, but there are no telephone connections in ICU. We do have a private calling area, but it is too soon for you to get up, even using a wheelchair, without first checking with the doctor. He will be making his rounds in about two hours, so you can ask him at that time," she replied with her beautiful smile. "Anything else, Mr. Ramos?"

"How long have I been here?"

"You have been here a week. You have been in a coma, and today is the first day you are awake."

"Has anyone visited me or called for me?"

"You will have to check with the doctor when he makes his rounds, but I have seen only one visitor. A gentleman did come and stayed only a short time. I didn't get his name, nor did I speak to him. I am sorry I can't help you more."

"Thank you. No problem. Thank you for taking care of me."

The nurse smiled and nodded. "Anything else, Mr. Ramos?"

"No, thanks."

The nurse did a last quick check of vitals and left.

Great, he thought. I have to get the doctor to let me use the telephone so I can reach Robert.

Alan had no idea if his CIA handler knew he was here or that he was even alive, but he doubted it. Alan drifted off again. He awoke, as someone was tapping him on the arm.

"Mr. Ramos, Mr. Ramos, can you hear me?" the man in the white coat was saying softly.

"Yes, yes, I can. Are you the doctor?"

"Yes, Mr. Ramos, I am your doctor—Doctor Santos. You have been in a coma for a week, and you have suffered a severe concussion injury, apparently from an explosion. You will be in ICU for at least three more days, and then you will have to go through a month of rehab. Fortunately, you are a young man and in very good shape, or you wouldn't be alive."

"Thanks, Doc, for saving me. I need to make a telephone call as soon as possible. Can you please let me use a wheelchair to make the telephone call?"

"I think you will be able to make a call tomorrow. By the way, a man who visited you asked me to call if you woke up."

"Did he give you his name?"

"No, he just wrote down his number and said to call him if you awoke."

"Can you wait and let me call him tomorrow when I feel better? I want to surprise everyone."

"Of course, Mr. Ramos. No problem. I will go get his telephone number from my office and bring it to you," the doctor replied as he now started to check Alan's chart.

"You are a very lucky man, Mr. Ramos. You are only alive because you were in top physical shape, and they got you into the hospital quickly. You had a serious concussion and slight damage to your lungs from a severe explosion. We didn't know if you would regain consciousness due to the severity of the concussion. How is your memory?"

"The memories are starting to come back but still not a hundred percent. Did you get the names of the men who dropped me off so I can make sure to thank them?"

The doctor looked slightly puzzled. "No, Mr. Ramos, they didn't provide their names. They just dropped you off at the emergency room. They seemed rather cold and businesslike about it all. They did arrange payment of your hospital costs."

"Thanks, Doc. I really appreciate all of you guys, and thanks for saving me. I think I will rest," Alan replied as the doctor smiled, nodded, and then left.

Alan woke up the next morning at 9:00 a.m. The nurse came in a short time later. "What is your name?" Alan asked as she walked in.

"Elsa. How are you feeling this morning? You look much better, and you are starting to get your color back. Do you still have strong pain?"

"I am okay. Got a high level of tolerance to pain."

"We noticed. The doctor asked me to give you this telephone number."

"I need to make a telephone call as soon as possible. The doctor said it would be okay this morning. Can you please help me?"

"Yes, Mr. Ramos, the doctor did leave a note on your chart that if you want to use the telephone, it would be okay. I will go get a wheelchair and be back shortly," she said as she left the room. In a short time, she was back. She helped Alan sit up and swing over to the wheelchair. She then hung the two drip bags and took off all his monitoring leads.

The telephone room was a short way down the hall. He saw several nurses looking surprised to see him up. The nurse placed him in the small room. "Press this button when you are finished, and I will come back and get you."

"Thank you so much," he said to the nurse as she left and closed the door.

Alan slowly picked up the telephone receiver and dialed the emergency number of his CIA handler, Robert. After the second ring, a man picked up the line and asked, "Who is calling?"

Alan sat quietly in disbelief that Robert had not answered the call. "I need to speak with Robert."

"Robert doesn't work here anymore. Who is this?"

Alan sat in complete disbelief and shook his head. "I need to speak to the person who has replaced Robert."

"No one has replaced Robert. I need to know your name to know how to direct your call."

Alan hung up the telephone and leaned back in the wheelchair. He was barely able to breathe.

I have got to get out of here as soon as possible, he thought.

Alan pressed the button, and in a few minutes, the nurse returned to take him back to his room. "I want to rest. I am tired. Please don't have anyone disturb me for the next two hours."

"No problem, Mr. Ramos."

Alan moved with the helping hand of the nurse back to his bed. The nurse reconnected his monitoring equipment and rehung the drip bags. She closed the blinds and turned off the light as she left the room.

Alan waited five minutes before he buzzed for the nurse. She came over to the bed.

"I would like to go to the bathroom. Can you help me?"

"I am not sure you are ready to walk, Mr. Ramos; I will need to check with the doctor."

Alan sat up in bed and swung his legs over the side. "I am ready, Elsa. Please help me," he said as he dropped to the floor.

The nurse rushed over with a rolling carrier for his IV bags. She shut off and disconnected the heart monitor and moved the IV bags to the carrier. When she finished, Alan was behind her and got her in a choke hold until she passed out. He pulled out the IV connections from his arm and carefully lifted the nurse into the hospital bed under the covers. He removed the heart-monitor attachments from his chest and placed them on the nurse's chest. He turned on the heart monitor, and it immediately began its steady, rhythmic beat.

Alan walked unsteadily to the door and carefully opened it to allow a view down the hall. No one was in sight. He slipped out the door in his hospital gown and ducked into a linen closet two doors down. He was light-headed but was functioning better than he hoped. He searched the racks and found a set of doctor scrubs, foot covers, and a cap and slipped them on.

Alan did a quick check out the cracked-open door; no one was in the hallway. He opened the door and walked down the hallway to the elevators. The nurse at the ICU station didn't even look up as he walked by. The elevator door opened, and two doctors got out, talking to each other, and he got in and pressed the button to the ground floor. The elevator door opened to the emergency room full of doctors, nurses, and patients. Keeping his head down, he walked slowly out the front door and onto the street. He knew this area of Cartagena; he was a mile from a safe house he had used in the past. He was still light-headed, but he was starting to feel the adrenaline he would need to get through the day.

# CHAPTER 2

## LAY OF THE LAND

Alan was exhausted when he reached the safe house. He was light-headed and dizzy. He crossed the street to the park across from the safe house and found an empty bench. He sat for ten minutes with his head in his hands, trying to stop the light-headed and dizzy feeling. For the next thirty minutes, he watched the safe house and looked for any signs of activity. All was quiet.

Slowly he crossed the street and walked around to the back of the house. He was on constant alert. The entry door was the back basement door. The push-button number lock looked exactly as it had the last time he was here. He pressed in the code: the address numbers, the current month, and the four digits of his month and day of birth. The lock opened immediately; the safe house was still set from his last mission.

The basement had a hidden interior wall door. Alan activated the door lock, and it opened. He now had clothes, weapons, cash, several forged passports, and IDs that had been placed at the safe house as backup for his last assignment. He strapped on a dive watch and picked up one of the Berettas. He checked the magazine. It was full, and he racked a round into the chamber. He loaded two more magazines in his pants pockets and picked out some clothes before moving upstairs. He carefully checked the entire safe house, and it was clear. He desperately needed food, water, and rest. The kitchen refrigerator had eggs, cheese, bacon, orange juice, milk, and coffee. Alan fixed an omelet and drank orange juice but no coffee. He needed sleep after he ate. He crawled into bed and was asleep immediately.

Alan awoke and looked at his watch. He had slept for four hours, and his head was feeling much better. He was now feeling more pain over his entire body, so he took four aspirin from the medicine cabinet. The door-lock opening would have sent notice to Langley that he had entered the safe house. He knew there was no remote video, but there was a closed video system inside the safe house. He dressed in dark-blue khaki pants, a polo shirt, and running shoes. He went down to the safe room and slipped on the Beretta holster with the silencer, picked out a UK and a Canadian passport, and slipped into his pocket five thousand US dollars in one-hundred-dollar bills.

It was time to call Langley and find out what was going on and what had happened to Robert. Alan dialed Robert's emergency number again, and the same man picked up.

"I would like to speak to Robert."

"Robert is no longer here. Please identify yourself."

"Agent Eighty-Seven Alpha. I repeat, Eighty-Seven Alpha."

"Please stand by while I get your protocol information."

"Roger that."

In three minutes, he was back on the line. "This is a secure line. What was your last rank in the army?"

"Marines, captain."

"What was the highest military award you received?"

"Silver Star."

"What are the last four digits of your agent ID number?"

"Five, three, one, six."

"Damn, Alan, we had you KIAed. You already got a star on the wall in Langley. The legend lives on; you have certainly lived up to your nickname again."

"Where is Robert?"

"Stand by. I have someone who will want to talk with you."

Alan waited for five long minutes before the line was picked up. "Alan, this is Eric Shultz. How are you?"

Alan leaned back in his chair, stunned and surprised. Mr. Shultz was the top guy of the Directorate of Operations for the CIA. Alan had met him several times in the past. "I am okay, sir. I was in a coma in a private hospital in Cartagena for seven days. I think the bad guys brought me there to see if I was going to recover. I am sure they wanted to interrogate and worse. Fortunately, I got out and made it to the safe house. What happened to Robert?"

"Robert took an early retirement after this mission. A tremendous amount of blowback occurred. I can give you the details when you get up here. I can't tell you how pleased I am to hear from you, Legend. I can't wait to hear and read the mission report. FYI, the entire top of that hill is gone. But first things first. We need to get you back safely to Langley. We will get back to you in the next hour. FYI, only one bad guy survived—the FARC battalion commander. He is in the Clinica San Fernando in ICU."

"Maybe I should pay him a visit, bring him some flowers and chocolates?"

"Are you up for an action before we extract you? He was a prime target as he put together the deal between the FARC communist insurgents and the drug cartel. We don't want him doing it again."

"Yes, I will be okay. Got to finish the mission, sir."

"If it was anyone else but you, Legend...okay, take a shot. Don't take any unnecessary risks. If you can't get to him, we can get him later."

"I will call as soon as I'm finished. Moving forward, what number should I use, and who should I work with?"

"Until you get back, just me. Let me give you my number."

Alan grabbed a notepad and pencil. "Ready."

Alan memorized the number and burned the notepaper. He sat quietly, deciding how to get this done. He picked up the telephone book and looked up the address of the clinic. He also looked up a medical-equipment-and-supplies store that would be nearby the clinic. He showered first, dressed, and then began working on his hair and beard. He added significant streaks of gray and silver that made him look ten to fifteen years older. He pulled out a pair of blue-tint contact lenses and carefully put them in. He did a double take at the mirror, as he looked very different. Finally, he pulled on the holstered Beretta with the silencer and a windbreaker and headed out the back door.

The medical-equipment-and-supply store was two blocks from the clinic. Alan purchased a doctor's coat, latex gloves, pen pocket protector, several pens, and a Holter EKG simulator. He walked the last two blocks to the clinic and carefully waited across the street for ten minutes at a bus stop while he watched the front door of the clinic. No visitors and only one doctor entered during this time.

Alan crossed the street and walked into the clinic. An elderly guard at the front desk was reading a newspaper and didn't look up. Alan checked the clinic map on the wall; the ICU was on the second floor. He took the stairs up. The ICU was at the end of the hallway. There were no guards or persons in the hallway, only a nurse at the nursing station.

"Hello, I am here to see Mr. Diaz. I have come a long way. We are family. Can I see him?"

"Mr. Diaz has been in a coma for the last week. Visiting hours aren't until three p.m., but since you have come a long way, and you are family, I will let you see him for ten minutes. He is in room two oh three."

"Thank you so much," Alan said as he moved down to the door. He carefully opened the door and checked the room. There was no one in the room but the patient in bed, who was attached to a heart monitor and drip bags. Alan walked over to the bed and examined Diaz. He had bandages around his head with light blood seepage. His right arm and right leg were in casts. The heart monitor was singing its rhythmic beat.

Alan pulled on latex gloves and carefully pulled the Holter EKG simulator out of the bag and checked the contact connections. He turned on the simulator unit and set it to a regular EKG, replacing one connection at a time. When he had replaced the last lead, he watched the EKG. There was no apparent change, and the EKG monitor was now operating completely independently of Diaz. He slipped the Holter simulator under the sheets next to Diaz. Alan picked up one of the pillows and placed it firmly over Diaz's nose and mouth. Diaz struggled only slightly, and in five minutes, it was over. Alan confirmed with a check of Diaz's pulse.

Alan carefully opened the door and checked the hallway. All clear. Alan again thanked the ICU nurse and said he would be back at 3:00 p.m. to visit again.

Alan called as soon as he got back to the safe house. "Well, now the mission is completed. I am ready to come home."

"Wow, that was fast," Shultz responded. "We have a car coming to pick you up. There will be two men—both Colombians but trusted CIA assets. You have now been reported missing from the hospital, and everyone is looking for you—cops, feds, and bad guys. Everyone. Our team will drive you twenty klicks south of Cartagena, and we will be extracting you by chopper."

"Excellent. Thanks, boss."

The pickup and extraction went without a hitch. Alan was picked up by Sea Stallion chopper, which was heading to sea to an offshore US Navy frigate. The chopper was coming back from a filed flight plan from a meeting between US Navy personnel and

Colombian Navy personnel. The pickup was quick and efficient—a hot landing and takeoff. Alan was delivered to sick bay, where the ship's doctor gave him a checkup and ordered rest. A day later he was flown into Port of Spain, Trinidad, where he caught a CIA Hawker 700B that would refuel in Miami and bring him to Dulles Airport. The aircraft had a doctor, nurse, and flight attendant. The doctor checked him out for a second time and had the same diagnosis. The doctor did find Alan had lost some hearing in his left ear, the side facing the blast.

In the air out of Port of Spain, the memories of the mission began to flood back over him. He still felt slightly light-headed. He grabbed a pad and pen and began writing up his mission report. The mission had begun perfectly. He had roped down from a chopper two klicks from the FARC communist insurgent base. The night had had a new moon. At 1:30 a.m. he had gotten inside the FARC communist-insurgent base barbed-wire perimeter after eliminating three sentries with a knife. He had been completely dressed in black with the SEAL night-vision gear, a black boonie, a black combat vest, and black combat boots. His face and hands had been covered with black and dark-green camouflage grease. He had a sixty-five-pound black field pack loaded with C-4 and remote detonators. He also had carried his folding-stock M-14 with a silencer with six extra magazines and his Beretta with a silencer and four extra magazines.

Alan had carefully and silently set C-4 at the two cocaine labs and the two large warehouses loaded with weapons, ammunition, RPGs, antiaircraft shoulder-fired missiles, and a very large quantity of military-grade explosives. His remote detonator allowed him to set off the C-4 at five-minute intervals in a specific order, beginning farthest from his planned escape and moving to the charges near the escape area, covering him as he left. He had just placed the charges in the last warehouse, when he saw troops moving toward him, taking cover as they approached. They knew he was there, and they were spreading out, looking for him.

Alan had moved to the area of the security wire, where he had planned his exit. He had carefully picked off the two sentries who were assigned to the area, with the silenced M-14. He had taken an area of cover behind a berm and just started to cut the wire, when the advancing troops opened fire with a withering cross fire. He just had time to cut the last of the wires. He had leaned around the berm area and picked off three of the closest troops, using his M-14 with a red dot sight. At the same time, he had set off the C-4 farthest from him, and the bright flashes and explosions were massive as the chemicals in the cocaine labs were set off.

Alan estimated he had been assaulted by at least forty-five troops armed with AK-47s. Fortunately, they didn't have night vision. The cross fire continued to be withering. He had known he could not hold them off; they would have flanked him and finished him off in the next twenty minutes. Alan had flipped his night vision and had surveyed the terrain outside the wire. With his infrared scope, he had found an area with large boulders. He knew he had to go. He had left his backpack and began a tight, irregular zigzag full run for the boulders fifty yards outside the wire.

The rounds had flown past as well as had hit all around him as he had run. He hadn't thought he could possibly make it, but if he had been shot, he would have just detonated all the rest of the C-4. He had run as fast as he could, and he had been able to reach the boulders without being hit. He had heard more and more rounds hitting the boulder; the rounds had started to come from the edge of the flanks. He had been well inside the last blast zone, more than one hundred yards inside, but he had no other choice but to detonate all the rest of the C-4. He had gotten as low behind the large boulder as he could and had pressed the detonator option for all the C-4 at once. The massive flash of light and the explosion and blast wave were the last things he remembered, until he woke up in the ICU at the hospital. He had no idea how he had gotten to the hospital and why they had not just finished him off.

Alan sat back and stretched, feeling weary to the bone, and ordered a Johnnie Walker Black on the rocks from the flight attendant. He finished his drink and slept the rest of the way to Miami, only waking up to land. Alan again slept from Miami to Dulles. A car was waiting to take him to Langley.

# CHAPTER 3

## TIME TO REBOOT

Alan used the eye scan to clear Langley security, as he didn't have his ID. He was brought directly to Eric Shultz, the top guy of the Directorate of Operations for the CIA. Alan waited for ten minutes before he was brought into the director's office. Eric was a small, wiry middle-aged man with thinning hair and was famous for his extraordinary intellect. Alan was surprised to see Robert, his handler, and Will Edwards, another CIA agent.

"Alan, I'm so glad to have you back here safe and sound. I understand the doctors have given you a clean bill of health except for some loss of hearing in your left ear."

"That is correct, sir."

"You are probably surprised to see Robert, after our previous discussion. I asked him to come in for this meeting."

Alan walked over, and Robert stood up, shook his hand, and gave him a brief hug. "Glad you made it, Legend; just one more close call. I wanted to come in and say good-bye as well as intro you to Will again. You may remember he was with me when I came back to get you on your yacht off Cat Cay in the Bahamas."

"Yes, I sure do. Will, good to see you again."

"First things first. You need to know the backstory of your mission. Looks like the Colombians had sent a warning. After the fiasco last year with the Colombians betraying us, Robert had given the Colombians the wrong date—three days later," the director began.

Alan turned and gave Robert the quick thumbs-up.

"Well, it gets worse after that," the director continued. "After your action, the Colombians, apparently in bed with the cartel, began a massive false public-relations campaign. They told the public the site of the massive explosion was a small village with women and children, with no drug labs or FARC troops or weapons. They claimed this was the result of an unapproved US-military air-action attempt to eliminate a drug lab, that the air-attack hit the wrong location. They beat us bad with this false PR program. Photos of the supposed village before, crying relatives on TV, newspaper headlines—it was a massive campaign. The blowback was massive. I was called into POTUS to brief him directly on the mission. Congress jumped on the bandwagon with many members who had been waiting for something like this to come after and bash the CIA. To stop the clamor in Congress, Robert had to retire."

"Wow. They just don't get it when they are used," Alan responded despondently.

"It's okay, Alan. I was willing and ready to be the fall guy. I was also in serious grief, as we were sure we had lost you as well," Robert quickly added.

"Roger that. I understand my star is already up in the lobby. Well, you can save it for the future," Alan said with a chuckle.

"Moving on, I asked Robert to come for your intro to Will. Will has been running the Absolute Resolution program in the Near East and Asia Pacific," the director said, pointing to Will.

"Alan, glad you made it. Good to see you again. I will be your handler moving forward," Will said as he walked over and shook hands with Alan. Will was in his forties, six foot two, in good shape, with gray and silver streaks in his brown hair that he no doubt had earned.

"Will is excellent. I have spent two days briefing him on you, and I know he will do an excellent job working with you. FYI—Will was also part of the Phoenix program at the same time we were in 'Nam," Robert confided.

"Alan, after this meeting, I want us to sit down and meet. I also want to buy you dinner tonight," Will said as they all stood up.

"Robert, hope you can do dinner," Alan quickly added.

"Wouldn't miss it," he said as they all shook hands with the director and headed down to Will's office.

Will asked his assistant to hold all calls, and he, Robert, and Alan sat down at the small conference table in the corner of Will's office.

"Well, let me say I am honored I will be working with you, Alan. Robert has given me your file and his own brief, and you certainly deserve your nickname, 'Legend.' This last mission has resurfaced you with the Russians, Colombians, and FARC insurgents as well. The Russians want you big-time, with the Cubans a close second. The FARC is a close third. Everyone is looking all over Central and South America for you. They got excellent photos of you while you were in the coma in the hospital, as well as your fingerprints. We are going to run a body scan on you tomorrow to make sure they haven't planted any type of tracking device on you. With all that said, we want you to take a break in operations in Central and South America for your safety. I am planning to use you in the Middle East and Asia Pacific for a while until things calm down in your previous assigned area," Will finished as he leaned back in his chair, waiting for Alan's reaction.

"Roger that. Completely understand," Alan immediately responded.

"Great. We got that off the table. We will, of course, miss you desperately; your Spanish is excellent, and no one has a better lay of the land in the Americas. I don't expect you will have a problem adjusting to the new operating area, and as an alias agent, that doesn't present a cover problem."

"Willing and ready," Alan replied.

They wrapped up their discussion and left together to go to dinner. They went to a French restaurant in Georgetown. Will ran over his past background, starting in 'Nam to the present. Alan was impressed, and he was surprised Will had been in Operation Phoenix and had not served in the military. He had come to 'Nam as a CIA spook but was still a field operative in 'Nam, running the same operations as Alan had completed.

They finished with a nightcap. Robert told Alan he needed to call Natalie, the black-ops-based London agent who had been Alan's partner on an assignment the previous year, as she had been told he had been KIAed. When she heard he had survived, she had asked to have Alan call her. Robert drove Will to his car and dropped Alan off at the Radisson in Langley. The next morning, Alan was back at Langley, where he had a body scan to assure no device or tracker was embedded on him. The thirty-minute scan determined Alan was clean. Alan dropped by to say good-bye to Will before heading to Dulles to fly back to Miami. "Can I use your phone to call Natalie?"

"Sure. I will leave you alone so you have some privacy."

Alan called the number Robert had given him, and an operator asked him to hold. After two minutes Natalie came on the line. "Alan, I am so glad to hear from you, mate!"

"Natalie, how are you?"

"I am great now; I was crying like a baby when I got first notice you were KIAed. I was sent a picture of your star in the lobby at Langley. I felt very guilty I had not taken off time before then to come see you. I realized how much I missed seeing you. I won't make that mistake again. When you get settled, call me, and I will fly over."

"You got it, mate. Sounds excellent. Take care of yourself and will call you in a couple of days."

"See you soon, mate."

Alan took a cab from the Miami Airport to the Dinner Key Marina. It was a beautiful day with a breeze. The boats were lightly rocking, and the rigging was lightly rattling. Alan stepped on his charter yacht and home, *Anne Bonny,* a forty-seven-foot Swan sloop. He unlocked the cabin and went down below and pulled a Red Stripe out of the refrigerator and climbed back up into the cockpit. This was a very long way from the hilltop in Colombia. He had used up another life; he had already far exceeded the fabled nine lives.

Working in the Middle East and Asia Pacific is going to be really interesting, he mused. I can't wait to see Natalie again; it has been too long.

# CHAPTER 4

## STRANGE BUT TRUE

The next morning Alan woke up as usual at 6:30 a.m. to the gentle rocking of the *Anne Bonny*. He had just sat up when his pager went off. It was Will, his new handler, requesting he call in. Alan slipped on a shirt and a pair of shorts, walked down to the main dock, and dialed the number using the pay telephone. Will answered on the first ring.

"Will, you paged me?"

"Yes, we've got an urgent assignment for you. Are you good to go?"

"Roger that. Are you sending me a package?"

"No, I need you to fly back up. Sorry for this quick turnaround, but we need to go over this mission in person. It is extremely delicate. We have a flight up booked for you in two hours out of the Miami Airport."

"Roger that. See you this afternoon."

The ticket was first class on Eastern Air Lines, and the flight was right on schedule. The car was waiting, and he cleared security and immediately went up to Will's office. Will's administrative assistant, Susan, led him directly into Will's office and closed the door behind her.

"Will, you certainly have piqued my curiosity."

"Alan, thanks so much for the quick turnaround. This came to me late last night, and it is considered critical and highly sensitive. You, me, the operations director, and the CIA director are the only ones cleared for access to this assignment."

"Wow."

"Once I brief you, it will be clear why. You are being authorized to eliminate two of the Contra leaders who are operating against the Sandinistas."

"You have got to be kidding. Aren't we funding those guys? I took out a finance guy years ago in Costa Rica for turning on the Contras."

"We are still funding them, but these two targets are really out of control. We have an independent trusted report they are working with drug cartels and have been identified and reported as having completed atrocious war crimes in Nicaragua. We created a couple of monsters; the director wants to eliminate them to prevent them from continuing as well as to send a message to the rest of the Contra forces. I think you understand how sensitive this is."

"I think that would certainly be an understatement. I am going to eliminate two guys whom we are funding?"

"FYI, I told the director we were shifting you to the Far East and Asia Pacific. He said he wanted only you for this one."

"Okay, when do I get the intel?"

"The director is deciding on one backroom guy to work with you. I will call up and see if he has picked the guy," Will said as he lifted the telephone and called the director. He had a brief conversation and hung up. "We got your man. He is heading up. It is the backroom intel and planning boss.

Within ten minutes, Frank Yates was shown in to Will's office by his admin assistant. Frank was in his late fifties, fit, and his hair was completely silver gray.

"Legend, great to finally meet you. I have heard a great deal about your service record. I will have your intel file completed tomorrow at zero nine thirty. Let's plan to meet tomorrow here in Will's office to review at that time. This mission is so sensitive, we're going to ask you to commit to memory the information you need. The top guy doesn't even want a burn paper file to leave Langley on this one."

They finished up, and Alan left and returned to the Radisson hotel in Langley. When he got to his room, he called Natalie. She picked up after he had a short wait.

"Alan, so glad to hear from you."

"Well, mate, got a business trip I have to complete, so you will have to wait to come take a sail."

"That is certainly quick. They are loading you back in the breach pretty quick, mate."

"I'll call you as soon as I get back, and hopefully you will have time to come visit. I can send you a ticket."

"Forget it, mate. Just take me sailing in the Bahamas. I will buy my own plane ticket."

"Call you as soon as I get back," Alan finished before saying good-bye.

Alan had dinner at the hotel and a drink in the bar before turning in for the night.

The car picked him up at 9:00 a.m. and brought him to the CIA office. He went directly to Will's office and was led right in. Frank was already there, and both were at the small corner conference table in his office.

"Coffee?"

"Thanks, Will. That would be great."

Will poured the coffee and passed the cup over to Alan.

"Well, I have completed a brief overview with Frank, and this is going to be a real tough one. Frank went over the intel with the

Directorate of Operations last night. He agrees. He said that was why he wanted only you."

"Well, I am flattered and concerned all at once."

Frank ran through all the data, passing the sheets one at a time to Alan to reread after Frank had given his overview.

"These guys are the commander and executive officer leading a battalion of Contras operating out of Costa Rica into southern Nicaragua. Most of their troops are ex-members of Somoza's National Guard and are reported to be seasoned fighters. The two targets were also in the national guard—a colonel and a captain."

Frank laid out the intel maps and U-2 aircraft photos for Alan to study. Will gave Alan an unmarked map of the area to take with him. Alan made some small pencil marks on the map and on a notepad as he worked out bearing and compass points.

"Well, how do you want this to look?" Alan finally said as he leaned back and stretched.

"The only priority is to eliminate these two guys. How and when you do it is your call on the ground. We can deliver to you whatever you want through our station in Costa Rica. Just make me a list, and we will have it ready."

"Guys, quite frankly this assignment is reminding me of the time before I quit on Operation Phoenix. There is really something inherently wrong when I am going to eliminate the unit leaders of a group we are funding."

"I know, Alan. This, of course, is troubling to all of us. I look at it as if we are eliminating two bad apples in a good program."

"Why would the troops in that unit follow them in war crimes? Isn't that an indictment of the whole unit?"

"We won't know that until we get rid of these two guys. We understand these two both rule with iron fists, and the troopers have no choice. Once these two are eliminated, we will see how this unit operates. If there are still problems with drug cartels and war crimes, we will take further action. Our hope is they will return to their mission: fighting the communists and taking back their county."

Alan leaned back in his chair and crossed his arms. Will and Frank could see Alan was not happy and was still struggling.

"Alan, eliminate these two guys, and then I promise we will carefully monitor this unit. I know the director is not going to let a US funded military unit commit war crimes or work with drug cartels. Our best intel tells us if we eliminate these two bad apples, the unit will return to its mission. We believe the number three and four officers are military professionals and will go back on mission."

"Okay. Not liking this at all, but I will get it done. How many more Contra units are we funding out there, acting as organized crime drug rings and committing war crimes?"

Frank and Will both sat quietly; neither said a word. The silence was deafening. They looked at the maps and photos.

Alan stood up. "I will have a list for you of what I will need before I leave. I will plan on flying into San Jose, Costa Rica, in three days and can meet the local station guy to pick up my equipment," Alan quietly advised.

Will and Frank stood up and shook Alan's hand. The both watched as Alan left.

"I was worried about this," Will said in a concerned tone. "Alan resigned from the Phoenix program in 'Nam when these types of things began happening."

"Let's hope he eliminates these guys, and this unit returns on mission. You can bet the farm Alan will be following up on the unit," Frank said as he shook hands with Will and headed back to his office.

Alan had Will's assistant, Susan, provide him a conference room, and he worked up the list of equipment he would require down in Costa Rica for the mission. When he was finished, he popped back into Will's office and provided him the equipment list.

Alan caught the flight back to Miami and wasn't back on the *Anne Bonny* until 10:30 p.m. He opened a Red Stripe and sat in the cockpit, enjoying the calm and peace of the night on the water.

Damn, this stinks, he thought. How in the world are we funding a military unit working with a drug cartel and committing war crimes?

# CHAPTER 5

## COSTA RICA

Alan flew into San Jose, Costa Rica, and the CIA contact from the San Jose station was waiting curbside in a dark-green Jeep Wrangler with a black hardtop. Alan jumped in the passenger side, and they took off.

"Lacy. Glad to meet you. I have only your alias name—Jim. Got all your gear in the back in a duffel. I need you to drop me off a mile from here, and I will be picked up. Here is your in-country pager that you can also use to send outgoing coded messages. We can only help you here if you are wounded and need help extracting. We can't help in the field for your mission operation. The codes are on the burn paper file; please burn once you have committed to memory the five key codes. Any questions?"

"So this Jeep has a private license plate. Who is it registered to?"

"It is registered to a land-surveying company that is part of your alias job cover. The insurance card is in the glove compartment as well. This is a CIA shell company we use to move in the backcountry. You have a transit level and a surveying rod in the back."

They drove to the drop-off spot and shook hands before Alan drove off. The five-speed shift was a little stiff but would be perfect if it was needed. Alan drove from San Jose to Los Chiles Caño Negro and checked into Hotel Castillo Tulipan, a local hotel with off-street parking. He paid cash for the week and, as typical, gave the front-desk clerk his passport; he had a second one just in case he had to leave without checking out.

He carried up his carry-on and the duffel from the back of the Jeep, as well as the land-surveying equipment. Once in the room, Alan checked the duffel and examined all the equipment he had ordered. He had everything he had asked for with double the ammunition he had requested. He removed the burn file with the codes and sat at the desk and rewrote each code at the bottom of the burn paper. He had a photographic memory of anything he wrote down. He was able to write down multiple pages and turn the pages in his head to review what he had written. He burned the codes once he had finished.

He went down and ate in the hotel dining room and had a steak with plantains and black beans and a glass of red wine. When he got back to the room, he studied the map to prepare for the next day.

*Day one*

Alan was up at 6:30 a.m. and completed his seventy-five push-ups. He went to the dining room and had bacon, eggs, and grits. He was dressed in dark-blue cotton slacks and a long-sleeved black T-shirt and carried the duffel and the survey equipment out to the Jeep and headed out east to Rio Infiernillo, twenty kilometers away on the back roads. He found the place he planned to park. He cut tree branches and camouflaged the Jeep behind a boulder ten yards off the road. The dark-green Jeep was difficult to see when he was finished. He moved fifteen yards, pulled out, slipped on his Beretta, silencer, and side holster, and racked a round into the chamber. He quietly waited for ten minutes, watching and listening. All was quiet; only the noise of jungle birds could be heard.

Alan was six kilometers from the Contra encampment that was deep in the rolling forested hills that led to steeper ridges and a single-canopy jungle. He outfitted all his gear. He pulled on his combat vest and loaded the six M-14 magazines and the four Beretta magazines. He grabbed his camouflage boonie and cut a handful of small branches to insert into the boonie rim bands and pulled it on. He applied the camouflage grease on his face and hands. He had a combat knife, his piano wire garrote with wooden handles, two frag grenades, and two smoke grenades. He also had his SEAL night vision as well as his FLIR target-range scope. At the bottom of the duffel was his M-14 folding stock and four claymore antipersonnel mines with the remote detonator as well as trip wires. He loaded the field pack from the duffel. He pulled the M-14 out and was surprised. He had lost his M-14 that he'd had since 'Nam in Colombia after the explosion. The equipment guys had built him a black, custom-made, folding-stock M-14 with the shortened barrel and a foregrip handle. The M-14 also had an auto-selector switch to allow semi- or full automatic. He checked the red dot sight, and it was fully operational. It was awesome. He racked a round into the chamber and set off for the Contra encampment in the steeper ridge area, stopping every ten minutes to watch and listen for any patrols that might be operating.

Alan reached the rock formation and the beginning of the jungle a kilometer from the Contra encampment. He began his careful approach by searching for the sentries. He picked up the two sentries covering the east side of the encampment. He could see the encampment; there were at least several hundred men visible, and the unit was definitely battalion strength. Alan took up a position and carefully examined the entire encampment with his FLIR scope. Sunset was two hours away.

The Contras had been sending regular nightly patrols across the border to raid any Sandinista military patrols and to win over the small villages that typically supported the Sandinistas. Alan planned to tail a patrol and do an "eyes on" of the actions the unit was conducting.

At 9:30 p.m., Alan could see that two ten-man patrols were gearing up and gathering in two groups for the patrol briefing. Alan listened to the briefing using his Super Ear listening device, designed solely for use by the CIA, which provided clear hearing of conversations. The commander provided clear, concise orders to cross the San Juan River into Nicaragua and head east down the river to intercept any Sandinista patrols and eliminate them. The patrol was to also talk to villagers and pass out fliers for support of the Contras.

At 10:00 p.m., the patrols moved out, and Alan carefully and quietly followed the patrol that was heading northeast. Alan stayed fifty yards behind the two-man rear-patrol security team.

The patrol crossed the San Juan River at a small pedestrian bridge with an empty Nicaraguan Immigration and Customs hut and no Sandinistas defending. Alan waited a full thirty minutes after the rear security team entered the jungle, before following them. Alan picked up their trail right away and again picked up the rear security team. The patrol was heading in the direction of El Castillo de la Concepción in Nicaragua.

Alan watched as the patrol spread out and surrounded a small village. Alan estimated the village to be three kilometers from Castillo de la Concepción. The patrol swept in from all sides into the village, consisting of six small houses. Alan took up a position that allowed excellent cover and a full view of the village. He re-checked the silencer on his M-14 and flipped down his night-vision gear.

The Contra troops began to kick in the doors of houses, forcing their way in. Alan could hear the screams of several women and a young girl. The village men were dragged out of the houses and held at gunpoint in the center of the village. The women's screams continued. Alan had had enough. He moved in position to be able to quickly take out the four Contra troops guarding the men. In seconds, he killed all four with quick head shots; they didn't have time to move or react.

Alan carefully placed his M-14 in his cover area and pulled his Beretta with the silencer and sprinted into the village. There were six more Contra troopers in the houses. He entered the first house and kicked in the door and found one of the Contra troopers trying to tear the clothes off a fighting and screaming woman, with the other trooper watching. Alan quickly shot the man assaulting the woman in the head, and the second man had just turned and started to lift his AK-47, when Alan put two rounds in his head. Alan pulled the woman away and pushed her in the bedroom. He then put one more round in the first man's head, before changing magazines and running out to the next house that had been broken into.

When he entered the second house, he saw the Contra troopers had dragged a woman and her teenage daughter to the bedroom and were trying to rip their clothes off. The woman and the girl were fighting furiously, and one of the Contra troopers hit the teenage girl, knocking her down. Alan had a clean shot at this first man but had to kick the second man away from the woman to get a clean head shot. He sprinted to the last house, and the two Contra troopers were holding down a woman and pulling at her clothes. Alan shot the closest man and then had a clear head shot a moment later on the second man. He put two rounds in his head after the Contra trooper had hit the woman and knocked her down.

Alan pushed the woman into the bedroom and jogged out to the center of the village. The women began to come out and were crying and hugging the men. Alan carefully and slowly approached them.

"I am here to help," Alan said in a quiet, calm voice. "I need your help to clean this up and to drag the bodies to the jungle to bury. We need to do a perfect job, so if they come back, they won't find the bodies or any blood."

The oldest of the men stepped forward. "Thank you so much for your help. We can bury their bodies in our small cemetery, and they won't be found. The women will clean up so there will be no signs of blood. What if they come back and use force or torture on us because of what happened to their men?"

"I will be around for a while. If they come back, I will be here." One of the women and the teenage girl came over and hugged Alan. Alan watched as the villagers buried the first two Contra troopers.

The old man was right; the Contra bodies wouldn't be found.

Alan checked the cleanup of the houses, and it was completed with no sign of blood left. The rags used in the cleanup were buried with the last two bodies.

The old man walked over and quietly said just to Alan, "This is not the first time they have come here and hurt the women."

"All of you should move north to an area protected by the Sandinistas. This area is too close to the Contras," Alan said with concern.

"We have lived here all our lives. Our fathers and grandfathers lived here. Our farmland and crops, how we earn our living and eat, are here," the old man said quietly and sadly.

Alan knew they would never leave. He said good-bye and picked up his M-14 and beat down a path in the jungle past the village, leading to the bank of the San Juan River. He double-tracked back on the trail to make it appear ten men had taken the trail past the village. He told the old man to tell the Contras if they came back that the patrol had passed through. Alan then proceeded back to the surveillance location he had set up near the Contra encampment and ate some MRE rations and drank a half quart of water. He napped on and off.

*Day two*

Just before daybreak Alan heard the other patrol come back into the camp and begin to unload their gear. The two top officers, Alan's targets, came out and met the patrol leader and had a discussion. Alan listened to them with his Super Ear gear. The patrol leader followed the two officers back to the command-tent fly area, where they reviewed maps. The patrol leader further reviewed in detail their patrol operation. This patrol had been uneventful.

At 9:30 a.m., another ten-man patrol began to gear up and gather near the command-tent fly area. Alan listened as they were briefed to search for the patrol that had not returned. This was surprising, as the Sandinistas had operated company-size sweeps in the area the day the patrol had disappeared.

Following this patrol in daylight was going to be a bigger challenge and danger for Alan. The patrol set off, and Alan stayed seventy-five yards behind the two rear-guard troopers, watching them by using his scope and following their trail through the jungle. The patrol reached the village, and the old man met them in the center of the village. He explained the soldiers had passed through but went on. The point man of the patrol called to the patrol leader, and the patrol moved out through the village on the trail Alan had created.

Alan followed the patrol until they reached the end of the trail at the riverbank. The patrol stopped and searched the area. They came together as a group and had a discussion. The point man pointed across the river and to the bank of the river near them several times. The patrol reversed and traveled back through the village and didn't even stop; they proceeded back to the encampment.

The Contra troops unloaded their gear, and the patrol leader headed to the command-tent fly. He spent close to an hour briefing the commander. Alan listened on his Super Ear listening device to their discussion. Finally, the patrol leader came out and headed to the mess area to eat.

Well, they certainly don't know what happened in the village, Alan noted. Will they go back? I can't take down the commander and his second-in-command until I know they aren't going back to the village.

Alan's pager went off on vibrate, and he checked the code. It was a Langley request to provide a status report. He sent back the code that he was in the field in the middle of the operation and could not call back for a status report. He got no pager response back.

*Day three*

The next morning a ten-man patrol was sent out to the east on the Costa Rica side of the San Juan River. They were obviously going to check the opposite side of the river, where Alan had created the tracks ending on the other side of the river. Alan didn't bother to follow this patrol, as he knew they wouldn't find anything. It was time to take out the commander and second-in-command.

The commander and the second-in-command were bunking together in a tent next to the command-tent fly. Alan took a nap, ate MREs, and drank a half quart of water. He waited, watching the sentries change out at 11:00 p.m. At 1:30 a.m., he started his approach into the encampment. He quickly took out two sentries with his combat knife from the side where he approached. The command-tent fly was empty, and he moved behind it to get to the rear of the tent, where the commander and second-in-command were sleeping. He waited for fifteen minutes at the back of the tent, listening for any sound from inside the tent. Not a sound. He used his razor-sharp combat knife to cut a slit to look in the tent with his night vision. He could see both men were asleep in their cots, which were in the center of the tent. Alan cut a long slit so he could slip into the tent. The tent was far enough away from the other tents that he would be able to use his silenced Beretta.

He approached the commander first and fired one close-range shot into his forehead. The second-in-command five feet away stirred with the slight whisper from the silenced round. Alan quickly stepped over and put one round into the side of the second-in-command's head. Alan then put one more round into each of their heads, before slipping out the cut in the back of the tent.

Alan made it back to his surveillance area without a problem. He prepared all his gear to move back to where he had hidden his Jeep. The extraction back to the Jeep went smoothly, and in a short time, he was driving back to Los Chiles Caño Negro and the Hotel Castillo Tulipan, arriving without incident.

*Day four*
He woke up at 7:00 a.m. and ate huevos rancheros for breakfast. The eggs were only in a clear sauce that was superhot, but Alan was starving and ate it all. He drove back to San Jose and stopped at a pay telephone to call the CIA station for the pickup of his gear and the Jeep. He picked up the CIA contact at a nearby gas station and gave him the keys and switched to the passenger seat. The CIA contact gave Alan his ticket and dropped him off at the Eastern Air Lines departure area.

Alan had time to call Will from a pay telephone. Will picked up right away. "Alan, glad to hear from you."

"Business trip went well. I will give you more details when I get back."

"Excellent. Travel safe."

Alan's ticket back to Miami was first class. It would definitely be a two–bloody mary morning.

Can't believe we are funding Contra units that are committing these types of atrocities, Alan thought. How many other Contra units were committing these types of war crimes and atrocities? This Contra operation was starting to feel like Operation Phoenix in 'Nam, where a good anti-insurgency operation morphed into a nightmare.

Alan could not stop thinking and worrying about the villagers. Alan wrote up his mission report on the flight. He would send it FedEx from the Miami Airport when he arrived.

# CHAPTER 6

## R AND R

Alan arrived back at the *Anne Bonny* at 7:30 p.m. He went down below and fixed a Dark and Stormy cocktail, ginger beer, and five-star Barbancourt rum with a slice of lime, and then he went back to the cockpit. Rain was moving in; you could smell it in the breeze. Alan zipped up several of the clear-side panels of the cockpit Bimini top so the cockpit cushions wouldn't get wet.

Damn, I can't stop worrying about those villagers, he thought. I know the Contras will be back again.

He finished his drink and turned in for the night without eating dinner.

At 6:30 a.m., Alan called Natalie from the pay telephone on the dock. He was put on hold for a short time, before Natalie picked up.

"Alan, so glad you are back. How was the trip?"

"Mission successful. Can you take some time and come across the pond?"

"Sure. Been waiting for you to get back. I already have the ticket, and I can leave tomorrow if that works."

"Excellent, mate. See you tomorrow."

Alan called Will next; he picked up right away. "Glad to have you back safe, Alan."

"Thanks, Will. The battalion commander and his second-in-command were taken out. I took them out in their tent while they were sleeping. The Contras in the unit will be sleeping with one eye open."

"Excellent. Let's hope this sends a message."

"Will, I have some real troubling news. I listened in on the briefing to two patrols by the commander and the second-in-command; all was straight-up military instruction. I followed one of the patrols, and they assaulted the villagers, attacking the women. I believe they did it completely on their own."

"What did you do?"

"I took out all ten of them," Alan replied in a steel-cold voice.

"Damn, Alan—you KIAed an entire patrol of the guys we are funding to fight the Sandinistas?"

"You're damn right I did, and I would do it again. Will, this is looking like Operation Phoenix in 'Nam when it went off the tracks and was a total FUBAR. That patrol was nothing but a bunch of vicious thugs and war criminals. We can't accept funding these types of atrocities and war crimes," Alan responded vehemently. "I have been worried sick about the villagers since I left."

"Calm down, Alan. I agree. We have a world-class FUBAR here. I need time to absorb this info and think this through. Take some time off. Unwind."

"I have Natalie coming over, and we plan to sail over to the Bahamas for a week. You and I have to talk about this when I get back."

"Roger that. I understand and agree. Let me go put out the fire of you taking out a ten-man patrol. Is it in your mission report?"

"Yes, the entire story. I sent it FedEx yesterday from the Miami Airport. You should have it this morning."

"Okay, I will handle this and think it through. We can talk as soon as you get back. You should probably plan on flying up, given the sensitive nature of this issue."

"Roger that. Call you when I get back."

The next morning Alan was waiting at the gate for the British Air flight to arrive from London. Natalie looked absolutely stunning when she came off the plane. Her white blouse and straight black skirt slightly above her knees was amazing on her statuesque five-foot-seven athletic frame. Her dark, curly hair was pulled back, and her big, blue eyes were sparkling. She ran over and hugged Alan. He picked her up and spun her around.

"Boy, are you a sight for sore eyes. You look beautiful, Natalie."

"You're looking good yourself, mate, especially with all you've been through. I like the new, small scar near your left eye. It makes you look even more like a sexy pirate," she said with a chuckle.

They took a cab back to the *Anne Bonny*, and Alan immediately began to get the yacht ready to get under way. Natalie went below and stowed her gear and changed into shorts and a bikini top. Alan had already backed the *Anne Bonny* out of the slip and had her under way out of the harbor, when Natalie came up with two Red Stripes. She looked absolutely fantastic. They set sail outside the harbor on a course to Cat Island.

The sail was excellent. Alan taught Natalie how to steer the yacht and maintain pressure on the sails and hold the course. She was a fast learner. They anchored at North Andros that night. Natalie pulled Alan down to the master's cabin. They didn't fix and eat dinner until an hour and a half later.

"Alan, do you want to talk about Colombia?" Natalie asked very quietly and carefully at dinner.

"Just a quick overview," Alan said quietly and provided a summary of the details.

"Wow, mate. That was a really close one."

"The last mission is the one that has me down," he replied and provided her with the details.

"Damn, how can the CIA keep funding groups doing these types of things? You need to drop this for now. I know you will address it when you get back," Natalie said as she stood up and pulled him up, wrapping her arms around him tightly, just holding him.

The rest of the trip was excellent. They swam and rented diving gear and dove several times. They just kicked back and relaxed and enjoyed each other's company. They caught and ate lobster every night they had dinner on the *Anne Bonny*. They both felt so comfortable together, and the sex was world-class. They took the dinghy ashore several nights to eat dinner, have drinks, and dance. Natalie was an awesome dancer.

When they docked back at Dinner Cay, Natalie packed up, and Alan took a cab out to the Miami Airport with her to catch her flight home. At the gate when boarding started, Natalie gave Alan a big hug and a deep kiss. "Well, mate, I had a wonderful time. See you again soon. You can bet on it," she said before heading to the boarding gate.

When Alan got back to the *Anne Bonny*, he sat in the cockpit, watching the early-evening sky and thinking.

Wow, I really love Natalie but in a way I've never loved before. This was not like my love for my lost Maria. Natalie and I have a unique relationship—love for the moment. No long-term commitment; we both know our next assignment could be our last. We are living love in each and every moment, without any other expectations.

Alan turned in for the night. He woke up several times with nightmares of the village women being assaulted and the villagers being executed.

# CHAPTER 7

## FUBAR

Alan woke up the next morning, ran for two miles, and did his push-ups. He showered and sat in the cockpit, enjoying the beautiful early-morning weather. He walked down the dock and called Will at Langley.

"Will here."

"Good morning. I am back. Natalie flew out yesterday. We had a great time. I needed this time off with her."

"Excellent. Sounds like it was just what the doctor ordered. I need you to fly up tomorrow. I want to review what is going on regarding the Contra mission."

"Have you checked on the villagers?"

"Yes. We can go over everything when you come. See you tomorrow," Will finished before signing off.

This answer caused Alan concern. It would have been really easy to say the villagers were okay. Alan had a bad feeling.

Alan caught the Eastern Air Lines morning flight and was at Langley at lunchtime. He cleared security and went directly to Will's office. Will's assistant let Alan know Will would be with him shortly. In ten minutes Will came to the door and invited Alan and closed the door.

"Sounds like you and Natalie had a great time. She is quite a woman; I would never want to cross her."

"You bet—it could be detrimental to your health. We had a great time. The time off with Natalie really helped me unwind after this Contra fiasco. Will, are the villagers okay?"

"Alan, I am sad to say the Contras executed the old man, the village leader, as he supposedly attacked one of their men with a shovel. No more details were given."

"That is absolute bullshit. If he attacked them with a shovel, they were abusing the village women again. Damn, Will, we can't just stand by while this is going on," Alan responded with controlled fury.

"Let me finish the brief. The captain who took over command of the Second Battalion contacted our Costa Rica stationman, who funds and provides their weapons, food, and ammunition. He told him that a ten-man patrol had disappeared and that the battalion commander and second-in-command had been brutally executed in their sleep. He said the troops wanted to know if this was Russians or Cubans and whether we could help him find out what had happened."

"So, what are we going to do? I want the villagers moved out of the village and given compensation for the loss of their land."

"Slow down, Alan. We are looking at the best way to handle this issue. The good news is they never did connect the villagers to the lost patrol. This is plenty complicated."

"Of course it is. We are funding and supplying thugs and war criminals. That patrol I eliminated was a good sample of that outfit. That entire unit is corrupt—thugs and war criminals. Ironically, the commander and second-in-command I eliminated may have been the only real professional military personnel. How did that happen?"

"It was interesting that the top Contra captain used 'Ghost,' your old radio call sign in 'Nam, to describe the person who did this. I did go back and check the translation; the Spanish word means 'ghost' or 'phantom,' so as in 'Nam, it was a good description for you."

"When will we have this resolved and those villagers protected? I can't live with what is going on there! We are better than this, Will."

"I'll buy you dinner. We'll be meeting with the top guy tomorrow to determine what we do moving forward. He wants your direct input on this."

"Roger that. Thanks, Will," Alan answered quietly.

The next morning Alan was at Will's office at 7:45 a.m. for the 8:00 a.m. meeting. They headed to the office of the director of the CIA. His assistant led them directly into the director's office.

Eric, the top guy for operations, was already sitting at the conference table in the office. The director came from behind his desk and walked over and shook hands with Will and Alan. "Great to see again, Legend. Sorry it is under these circumstances."

"Well, let me open the discussion. Alan, I read your mission report. It, of course, was very disturbing. I have asked you, as well as Will and Eric, to discuss this issue. Will has told me of the level of distress this has caused you. I wanted to meet for us to discuss the issue and find a resolution. Eric, can you start us off?" the CIA director began.

"Yes, sir. I, of course, reviewed Alan's report and felt sick thinking we were funding and arming these thugs. We all have experience in 'Nam on this type of behavior. POTUS very much wants to support the Contras. I will be very interested to hear from Alan."

"I also would want to hear from Alan, who was on the ground, before I comment," Will responded when it was his turn to speak.

The three men turned to Alan.

"I have given this a great deal of thought and also have been haunted by what has and may happen to the villagers I personally met. I know the Contra support is by order from the top. I still believe we can prevent these types of war crimes. I recommend I go back down and travel with the station agent directly, handling the funding and arms to each Contra battalion. Let them know we are getting reports of war crimes, and we want to make sure they stop. I can start with the units operating out of Honduras so we don't flag the unit in Costa Rica that could endanger those villagers," Alan said, leaning back and pausing to get a read on the other men.

"Go on, Alan," the CIA director replied.

"Word will travel quickly, so the Costa Rica battalion will hear about our visits and should believe this issue was tripped by the units in the north. I would advise each unit that we would be carefully monitoring their operations, and any units found committing war crimes would have their funding, arms, and ammunition stopped." Alan finished and again leaned back.

"I like the concept, Alan. Of course, we may not actually be able to stop funding and support, but we can certainly threaten we will. Will and Eric, your thoughts?" the director said, turning to the other two men.

"I like it a lot. I feel the same as Alan. We can't close or eyes or turn our backs," Eric quickly responded.

"I am all in," Will quickly followed.

"Okay, we have an action plan. Given the nature of this, I won't be elevating this up. We have to allow deniability. I will leave this in Will and Alan's hands. Eric, make sure they get whatever they need. I want only the top guy from the back room, who already worked with Alan on the first project, involved. I want to keep this a very small circle," the director said as he stood up. They all shook hands, and Eric, Will, and Alan left. Outside the director's office, Eric shook hands and left for his office. Will and Alan returned to Will's office.

"I want to take Rene with me. He and I have been working together since 'Nam Operation Phoenix. He was a sheep-dipped

SEAL. We just worked on an assignment last year. He is based out of the station in Port-au-Prince, Haiti. He speaks Spanish fluently."

"Absolutely. I want someone who can watch your back. I know Rene, and I saw the work you have completed together in the past in your file. I want you to go down and meet with Frank Yates, the head of backroom intel and planning, to review what you will need to visit each of the units and locations of the Contra battalions operating out of Honduras and Costa Rica."

Alan met with Frank and reviewed all the positions and station contacts. He was given maps for each location. Alan requested full gear to support three weeks of field operation, so he and Rene would have backup supplies if needed. Alan finished up and went back to meet with Will. They called Rene, and he was ready to go and would fly up to meet Alan in Miami, so they could fly into Honduras together. Everything was set.

"Will, thanks for your support on this issue. It took me years to recover from the end of my assignment with Operation Phoenix in 'Nam. I vowed to myself to never just walk away if something like this happened again."

"Alan, all of us support you one hundred percent. We are all thankful you went on that first mission and found out firsthand what was happening. There were, of course, rumors and stories but no hard evidence. We need to fix this. We are better than this."

Alan departed and picked up his ticket and was dropped at Dulles. He flew back to Miami and was back at the *Anne Bonny* at 7:00 p.m. He pulled a Red Stripe from the refrigerator and went back to the cockpit.

I didn't expect this support, he thought. Having Rene on my six will be awesome. I'm going to stop these atrocities. I am not going to walk away again like Operation Phoenix in 'Nam.

# CHAPTER 8

## HONDURAS

René was waiting at the gate at the Miami Airport when Alan arrived. Rene walked over, and they gave each other a fist bump, pulled their hands back opening like an explosion, and crisply saluted. They had been doing this since 'Nam. Alan gave him a brief hug.

Rene was a mountain of a man at 6 foot 2 inches and 225 pounds and was in top athletic shape. He was Cajun from southern Louisiana, as well as part black and part Cherokee. He was sporting a military haircut. He looked, and was, very dangerous. Rene had been a SEAL in 'Nam before he was sheep-dipped into the CIA for Operation Phoenix. For a year, he was Alan's partner in Operation Phoenix, before Alan walked away.

Alan and Rene boarded the Eastern Air Lines flight. Both had first-class seats. The nonstop flight to Tegucigalpa, the capital of Honduras, was four hours, and Alan and Rene barely spoke. They, of course, would never discuss a mission on a commercial aircraft. Alan was reading a Buckminster Fuller book, and Rene listened to music on his Philips cassette player with earphones. They also played a game of chess on Alan's portable metallic chessboard at the same time. When it was time to land, the chess game was a stalemate.

Alan and Rene had carry-ons, so they proceeded to the pick zone for passengers. A green Jeep was waiting, the driver holding a placard with Roberts, Alan's alias cover name. They loaded their bags and climbed in the Jeep.

"Alan and Rene, glad to meet you. Phil Hendricks, local station agent, and I handle the two Contra battalions in Honduras. I have all your gear in two duffels in the back. Your cover is employees for a land-surveying company. I have all your ID info in this envelope," he said as he passed Alan the envelope and pulled away from the curb. Alan took his cover ID and company badge and passed the envelope back to Rene.

"I am going to take you to the Hilton to check in. Alan, I have you booked in a suite, so we will have room to meet. We will head out in the morning to visit the encampment of the Contra First Battalion."

They arrived, checked in, and went up to the rooms. They met shortly after in Alan's suite.

"Damn, how come you got the suite?" Rene chuckled.

"It was random, Rene—no slight," Phil said, suppressing a laugh.

They sat around the table and laid out the maps and information packets. Phil went over the encampment and surrounding areas and then reviewed in detail the background of the entire chain of command as well his impression. He was knowledgeable and a tremendous help in bringing Alan and Rene up to speed in a short time. They wrapped up, and Phil left the individual folders for each of the Contra key command-chain personnel for Alan and Rene to review in detail. They spent the rest of the night studying the individual folders, only taking a break to go down and have dinner and a glass of wine.

The next morning Phil picked up Alan and Rene at 6:00 a.m., and they headed for the Contra First Battalion encampment near the Nicaragua border in a jungle area. The sentries on the back-road into the camp waved Phil right through. Phil pulled up in a vehicle-parking area, and they got out and walked over to the command-tent fly cover in the center of the camp.

"Jorge, good to see you. Here are the two gentlemen I told you about," Phil said as he walked up and shook hands with the battalion commander. He was in his forties with dark-brown hair and in good physical shape. Both Jorge and his second-in-command looked every bit a battalion commander and executive.

"Gentlemen, welcome to the headquarters for the First Battalion. Phil has advised me of the reason for your visit. Please come over to this table, and we will be glad to sit down and discuss our operations," Jorge replied as he led the men back to the table in the rear of the command-tent fly.

Alan formally introduced both himself and Rene and explained they were from the Inspector General's office of the CIA. Both Alan and Rene pulled out their IDs, and the commander only briefly looked, before they began their discussion. After a full hour, Alan asked to randomly interview a company captain, the battalion sergeant major, and four random troopers. Without hesitation, the commander set up the interviews and left while the interviews took place.

When those interviews were complete, the commander reviewed their combat-operations maps and an overview of their last five operations. Alan and Rene were both impressed. The commander was a pro, as was the executive officer. Alan stood up and shook hands and thanked the commander and the executive officer for all their help and signaled Phil they were ready to go.

Once they had driven out of the encampment, Alan was the first to speak. "Those guys are pros, completely checked out. I still want to drive across the border and use our United Nations cover to talk to the villagers and close the door on this outfit as clean."

They drove across a bridge that crossed into Nicaragua and easily cleared the Sandinista Immigration and Customs using their UN IDs, UN magnetic signs on the Jeep doors, UN armbands, and baseball hats. They drove to three nearby villages and talked to the villagers on their issues and how they were treated by the Sandinistas and Contras. The villagers clearly favored the Sandinistas but also mentioned the Contras had provided food and medical supplies.

They drove back into Honduras and noted several of the Contra troopers watching down the road as they drove by with the UN signs still on the Jeep's doors. They drove back to the Hilton and ate before going up to the suite.

"Those guys are absolutely clean. I will sign off on them. Your thoughts?" Alan started the discussion.

"Roger that. I agree a hundred percent," Rene replied.

"I felt good about these guys, and I'm glad they checked out. You guys did a real complete and fair review. We are set up for the same agenda for tomorrow with the Third Battalion," Phil said, before getting up and saying good-night. Alan and Rene went down and had a glass of Pinot before turning in for the night.

The next day, the visit with the Third Battalion and the villagers in Nicaragua was almost identical. The unit was led by military pros, and all the interviews went well. The villagers echoed the sentiments of the previous villagers. Alan, Rene, and Phil returned to the hotel for a final meeting.

"Phil, you are running a clean operation. We will sign off on both your units. I am regaining hope. I know we have one bad apple—and I hope only one. What do you know about the two battalions operating out of Costa Rica?" Alan asked carefully.

"Alan, I want to be careful. I prefer to have you go in with an open mind, with the exception of the Second Battalion, which you know for a fact. I hope you understand, as Ed in Costa Rica is a friend and a good man. I understand you met him when you were down before."

"Yes, I did. He was an up-front guy and, of course, reported and arranged the hit on the Second Battalion commander and executive officer. I more than understand. We will go in open-minded on the Fourth Battalion," Alan said as he stood up.

"I will drive you guys to the airport in two hours. There is a flight tonight at twenty-two hundred hours that will get you into San Jose in an hour. Ed will be waiting to pick you up," Phil said before he left.

The flight was on time, and Ed picked them up and dropped them at the Hilton Hotel. The schedule was to spend the next day reviewing intel and personnel files for the two Costa Rica-based Contra battalions. They would visit the Fourth Battalion the following day and the Second Battalion last. This time Rene got the suite. Alan and Rene went down and had a couple of glasses of Pinot and caught up on personal issues.

# CHAPTER 9

## BACK IN COSTA RICA

They met in Rene's suite at 8:00 a.m. Ed brought a large legal briefcase with all the intel and personnel files. They sat down at the table with cups of coffee and began their review. They spent all day reviewing the files and intel for an early start the next day.

They started with the Fourth Battalion and were finished in three hours. Everything appeared in order.

Ed carefully collected and placed the Fourth Battalion intel and files on the floor and started to pull out the intel and personnel files on the Second Battalion. Alan and Rene began their review, and Ed poured everyone more coffee. After an hour, Alan leaned back and whistled.

"Wow, how did we end up with this crew, Ed?" he asked quietly.

"It is a long story, but I will give you the quick overview. You will remember Congress cut off our funding in 1983. We had created the First Battalion a year before without any problems. In fact, we had quite a few rank-and-file troopers left but no senior officers, no company commanders, and only a couple of NCOs. This was right when the funding was cut off," Ed said quietly and leaned back to watch Alan and Rene. They didn't say or ask anything.

"I thought I was going to be pulled out. I was surprised and shocked when I was told to carry on and do the best I could with the funds I had left. I was down to less than a half-million dollars, and I had to send half to Phil to keep the First Battalion operational. At the same time, there was a new adviser, an army colonel, guy named West, now working with our National Security Agency contact. They were putting extreme pressure on all of us, especially me, to get a Second Battalion up and operational. The result is the personnel files you just got finished reviewing," Ed finished with obvious concern.

"Wow, what a bunch of losers in this unit," Rene responded. "What happened after this gang of losers was assembled?"

"Well, that was when everything changed. Suddenly, we were receiving more funding than before Congress cut us off. I have no idea where the funds were coming from, and Colonel West told me the funds were coming from people and countries that supported the Contras. It, of course, didn't seem right. The funds, weapons, and ammunition were coming through very questionable arms dealers we had never dealt with before. The NSA contact and Colonel West said there was no issue with us providing guidance and advice to the Contras, and this was simply disbursing funds from third parties. The whole thing stank to high heaven."

They all sat quietly for several minutes.

"So that is why the Third and Fourth Battalions were quality units—you and Phil had sufficient funds again to properly recruit and operate. Why didn't you disband and rebuild the Second Battalion?" Alan finally responded.

"I was told not to. I was told it was critical to have as many fully functional battalions as possible. I clearly went on record multiple times that I didn't consider the Second Battalion to be 'fully functional' as well as dangerous to the Nicaraguan civilian population. I was overruled," Ed replied, obviously disgusted. Rene just shook his head.

"I came very close to quitting and discussed quitting with my boss. This is when Colonel West came up with the brilliant idea to eliminate the commander and executive officer as a warning to the unit. These guys were top-notch; I fought for days to stop this plan without success. I recruited these two guys; both were military professionals and graduated from our Officer Candidate School. I was also told not to mention this to whoever came to take care of the wet work mission," Ed finished with obvious disdain and frustration.

"Son of a bitch…I remotely listened in on the commander and executive's discussions and orders. I felt they were professional. Damn; I should have gone with my instincts and not taken them down," Alan replied with both anger and remorse.

"Don't beat yourself up. You only had a short time and explicit orders," Ed replied quietly. "Colonel West also insisted on designating the new commander and XO after you eliminated the other two. These guys are no good—again, criminal records but with military experience. I strongly disagreed, and West overruled me."

"Okay, we are where we are. The real question is, what is the solution to a dysfunctional battalion full of misfits and criminals working with a drug cartel?" Rene finally responded.

"This is the sixty-four-thousand-dollar question," Ed said as he stretched and leaned back in his chair. "The powers that be want this battalion, despite the fact that I have reported numerous occurrences of proven war crimes, atrocities, and drug smuggling and trafficking," Ed said with obvious frustration.

"Okay, let's do the fieldwork to document everything. Then it will be time to deliver this information to the top guy," Alan replied as he stood up. "I need a lunch break."

"The NSA guy and Colonel West aren't going to like this," Ed said, unable to hold back a smile.

"Fuck 'em. We are down here at the direct orders of the director of the CIA," Alan quickly responded.

"Fair warning. Reportedly, the NSA guy and Colonel West have the ear of the chief of staff for POTUS," Ed replied cautiously.

"Noted," Rene said in a steel-cold voice.

They finished their review, and Ed left. Alan and Rene went for a three-mile run and then an hour at the gym before having an early dinner. They played one game of chess, which Alan won. They finished with a glass of Pinot before turning in early for a long next day.

They left early morning for the Contra Fourth Battalion encampment. They used the exact process as Alan and Rene had used in Honduras. The review took a little over four hours. Both Alan and Rene were impressed, and the unit was staffed with well-trained and experienced officers and, more importantly, noncommissioned officers. They visited the nearby villages in Nicaragua and found there was slightly more support for the Contras than they had found in the north. The Contras were providing food, medical supplies, and doctors visiting the villages on a regular basis.

"This outfit looks tight. I like the number of experienced NCOs. The commander and executive officer were both top-notch graduates from US Ranger School. They also are doing a very good job of winning hearts and minds," Alan said once they had finished.

"I agree a hundred percent. These guys look tight and well trained," Rene responded.

The next morning Ed picked up Alan and Rene at 6:00 a.m. Rene, sitting in the back seat, pulled out Alan's and his Berettas with their shoulder holsters with the silencers. They slipped them on and pulled their windbreakers back on after both racked rounds into the chambers.

"Got yours, Ed?" Alan asked.

"You bet. Never go to the Second Battalion without it," Ed immediately responded.

The drive was four hours, with was much off-road and back roads. They passed the spot Alan had parked his Jeep and camouflaged it. This time they continued to drive down the road and were signaled through by the sentries on the road. They parked in the vehicle-parking area and proceeded to the command-tent fly. The new commander and executive officer were waiting for them.

"Ed, good to see you. These must be the two men you told me about," the commander said.

"Yes, Rodrigo, these are the two gentlemen from the inspector general's office of the CIA," Ed said as he completed the intros using Alan and Rene's aliases.

They all shook hands and moved back to the table at the rear of the tent fly. "I have been hearing from the other commanders on the process you are using for your review. I have no problem, but I highly recommend you not cross into Nicaraguan territory, as we are seeing aggressive actions by the Sandinistas. We lost a ten-man patrol not long ago; we never even found their bodies," Rodrigo began the conversation.

"Thanks for the warning. We will begin with the interviews. We want to interview three captains, two NCOs, and six troopers," Alan responded, pulling out his notepad.

"We will get them for you," Rodrigo replied as he signaled his executive officer. Alan, Rene, and Ed spent the next three hours interviewing. Rodrigo didn't leave. He sat and listened to all the interviews. The responses during the interviews were very apparently coached and in almost every case rang false. They finished up and spent the next hour reviewing the battalion-operating areas on the maps and the last five operations. There was no mention of providing food, medicine, or doctor services to the Nicaraguans. They wrapped up their meeting, shaking hands with the officers, and drove away.

"What a bunch of manufactured bullshit," Rene finally said after ten minutes. They were all thinking the same thing.

"That is why this time I didn't ask for random interviews. I think we just interviewed the key players. I let the commander pick the interviewees, and he did exactly what I expected: he made sure we talked only to the crew that would cover for them."

Alan pulled out the map and showed Ed the village as well as the other two villages he wanted to check using their UN cover. They stopped a half mile down the road and stored their Berettas for the border crossing and put on their UN cover gear. They had no problem crossing the border, where the Sandinista troops were handling Immigration and Customs.

They drove directly to the village where Alan had taken out the Contra patrol first. The villagers came out of their houses and stopped their work to walk over and meet the Jeep in the center of the village. Ed, Alan, and Rene got out, and Alan asked to speak to the village leader. The teenage girl Alan had saved began to shout. "Mom, this is the man with the green face who helped us. I remember the way he speaks," and she ran over and hugged Alan. "They killed my grandfather after you left. He was trying to save my mother."

Two men walked over to Alan, Rene, and Ed and advised that they were now the village leaders after the elder leader had been killed by the Contras. They spent time reviewing the execution of the village elder, who had attacked a solider attacking a woman with a shovel and was killed. Numerous raids and attacks that had occurred on the village since Alan had left.

"We are working on a solution for you as soon as possible. We will come back soon," Ed said as they loaded in the Jeep.

The next two villages were the same story, except in one village they had executed two men and taken one of the village's teenage girls, and she had not been seen since. Her mother and father were beyond consoling.

They finished at the last village and headed for the border and crossed without any problems. There was complete silence in the Jeep for over an hour. Alan knew they were all feeling and think-ing the same thing. Finally, Rene said quietly, "These guys are out-of-control monsters and have to be stopped and eliminated, period."

"I knew it was bad, but I had no idea it was this bad. I think I didn't want to know how bad it was, as there wasn't anything I could do about it. I am going to miss a lot of sleep over this," Ed said with remorse.

"Let's get this written up when we get back. I want one hundred percent complete agreement on the report, so we all need to work on it together. Ed, please make us reservations back to Langley tomorrow morning. I got to get out of here before I go back and start shooting those lousy bastards," Alan said with barely controlled rage.

When they got back to the hotel, they had an early dinner and sat in Rene's suite, drafting the report. The summary took over four hours to finish with consensus, as they all knew the top guys often read only the summary. Alan and Rene were shocked at the reports Ed had previously sent on the drug-smuggling activities he had documented and that nothing had been done. They assembled the detailed backup for the summary and finished at 11:30 p.m. The final document was the most damning collection of information that Alan and Rene had ever seen against a military unit.

"Ed, what is the story on the CIA's complete lack of action on all these atrocities?" Rene finally asked.

"Well, I believe it is all being kept quiet and in the dark by Colonel West. My reports all go directly to him."

"Your CIA boss isn't getting copies of your reports?" Rene asked in disbelief.

"No. Only Colonel West gets my reports. He then is creating a report for the CIA and the NSA. I don't get to see them. I believe this guy's only priority is to be able to say he has four battalions of Contras. I don't trust this guy. FYI, he is the guy who has come up with the alternative funding. Be careful of him when you are back there," Ed said with disdain and grave concern.

They all agreed they needed a drink—several of them. They went down to the hotel bar and then to a quiet corner table with their second neat single malt Scotches.

"I won't stop until this is fixed," Alan toasted, and Ed and Rene both gave a "Hear, hear!"

# CHAPTER 10

## BACK AT THE PUZZLE PALACE

Alan and Rene caught the morning flight out of San Jose through Miami and arrived at Dulles in the late afternoon. They went directly to Will's office.

"Alan and Rene, great to have you guys back safe and sound. I was surprised you didn't send your report ahead," Will said with concern.

"We thought we should present it in person. It is shocking. We wanted to make sure we could immediately address any questions that came up during the preliminary review. Will, this is far worse than I imagined," Alan responded.

All three men sat quietly for several minutes. "Okay, give me the Cliff Notes version so I can then do a full review," Will finally replied.

"Rene, why don't you start?" Alan said as he turned to Rene.

"Sure. Will, we got a major problem, and it is deeper than a rogue battalion. A better description may be a colonel problem. Do you know the NSA guy, Colonel West?"

"I haven't met him, but certainly I have heard about him. I understand he is the NSA lead on the Contra program."

"He sure is. Did you know Ed's reports in Costa Rica on the Contra program go directly to Colonel West without a copy to CIA headquarters?" Rene carefully questioned.

"No, that is not possible. The reports also have to be coming back here as well."

"Well, Will, Ed has told us his reports go only to Colonel West, who then creates a report that is sent to the CIA and NSA," Rene shot back.

Will pushed back his chair and leaned back. His look clearly showed his level of surprise and disbelief. He sat quietly for a full minute.

"That does not seem possible. But if Ed has told you this, then he certainly would know better than anyone else," Will finally responded. "But this certainly explains the disconnection between the internal reports and the third-party allegations. I know Ed and had worked with him in the past. He is a straight shooter. This was the reason we sent you and Alan down for an independent look. Let's get into the details you found now."

Alan and Rene spent the next forty-five minutes reviewing their report summary, providing more detail in response to Will's questions. They could both see Will was shocked and surprised. When they finished, they all again sat quietly for several minutes, with Will and Alan leaning back in their chairs and Rene with his arms crossed.

"So what are your ideas for solution for the Second Battalion problem?" Will finally asked.

"This may be the simple part of this FUBAR. I eliminated the wrong guys when I took out the commander and executive officer. Damn upset about that. The new commander and executive officer are definitely bad guys brought in by Colonel West. They also gave us a random sample of officers, NCOs, and troops—who clearly are also bad guys—to make sure we heard the same story in the interviews." Alan began to lean back, waiting for Will's response.

"Sorry on the two good guys you took down; we can address that next dealing with Colonel West," Will said, waiting for Alan to continue.

"The Second Battalion solution is simple. We need to eliminate the bad guys we identified in the battalion. That leaves the battalion intact but allows Ed to rebuild the leaders of the battalion who can straighten out the entire unit as he did it with the Fourth Battalion—no intervention by Colonel West. I will run through my proposed plan with the backroom guys," Alan stated quietly, "but I want to be there when it happens."

"Okay, I will now need to set up a meeting with the top guy at Operations and the CIA director," Will said as he picked up his telephone and asked his assistant to check on the availability of both men. Within minutes, she rang back and advised they could meet with both men in thirty minutes.

"We will have to hear what they have to say about Colonel West. The ball is in their court on that one," Will said as he picked up the report documents before they headed up to the CIA director's office.

They waited only a few minutes, before they were ushered in and led over to the conference table. Eric, the top guy in Operations, was already there and stood up and was introduced to Rene and shook hands with Alan and Will. The CIA director hung up his telephone, came over, and was introduced to Rene and shook hands with Alan and Will. Will provided the director and Eric the report summary, and Alan went over the key details.

"Alan, thank you for taking this assignment in the first place, and both you and Rene for your excellent follow-up. It has been a real eye-opener and, quite frankly, has really opened up a can of worms. We found out a great deal of information we were not privy to and still have a lot more questions," the CIA director said, pausing to see if there were any initial comments. Everyone sat very quietly, carefully listening.

"We have many issues to deal with now," the CIA director continued, "but the most important issue is to make sure we stop the war crimes, atrocities, and drug smuggling being carried out by the Contra Second Battalion. I am worried sick about the villagers, as I'm sure you all are. Alan, do you have a plan?"

"Sir, all I know is, the players we have identified have to be eliminated. I will certainly volunteer to finish this mission. I can work with Ed from backroom planning to come up with the operation plan. I expect the plan will be we simply need to take out the bad players, as the opportunity arises, as in the Phoenix program in 'Nam, over a two-week period," Alan replied, waiting for feedback.

"I volunteer as well," Rene immediately jumped in.

"Thanks, Rene. Will and Eric, your thoughts?" the director said, leaning back in his chair.

"I agree one hundred percent," Will replied.

"Me too," Eric followed. "It makes sense and allows Ed in Costa Rica to rebuild the Second Battalion without loss of the unit. But we need to make sure Colonel West has no input in restaffing."

"Okay, you can go down to planning after this meeting and meet with Frank, the top planning guy only, and plan this out and tell him you get whatever you need," the director said quietly.

There was total silence for the next two minutes; everyone was thinking the same thing.

"What about Colonel West?" Alan finally said.

"Alan, believe me when I tell you your first findings started further investigations, and the Second Battalion issue is the tip of the iceberg. Unfortunately, you, Will, and Rene didn't have clearance at this time to further discuss Colonel West. Trust me when I tell you we are most certainly pursuing this matter," the director said with obvious concern, leaning forward.

No one spoke again for several minutes.

Eric stood up first. "Hope you guys understand. No doubt in the future, you will see firsthand what transpires. But right now, it is all dark."

Will, Alan, and Rene all stood up and shook hands before heading out. Eric remained with the director.

Will, Alan, and Rene went directly to backroom planning and asked for Frank. He came out of his corner office and invited them in. They ran through the mission and objectives. Frank took extensive notes and advised he would have a game plan ready by ten the next morning.

Alan and Rene said good-bye to Will after the meeting and headed over to the Radisson in Langley, where they were staying. After checking in, Rene came up to Alan's room.

"What the hell do you think is going on with Colonel West?" Rene asked as soon as he closed the door.

"I bet it is the funding. Ed in Costa Rica said he was getting funds, weapons, and ammo from some very shady guys. Suddenly he had all the money, weapons, and ammo he needed. This unlimited flow started three months after Congress had cut off funding to the Contras. I don't believe in coincidences. The question is, where is Colonel West getting this type of third-party funding? He told Ed that it was other nations as well as individual supporters of the cause," Alan said, crossing his arms and leaning forward in his chair.

"You are probably right. Wow, the director sure seemed to indicate it was a real major FUBAR."

"Let's go have a drink. I need one," Alan said as he stood up and moved to the door.

"I need two," Rene said as he followed him out.

The next morning Alan and Rene met with Will and Frank from planning. He laid out multiple options for Alan and Rene to choose. Alan and Rene ordered gear to cover three of the five options, and they wrapped up the meeting.

"Alan, you guys keep me up to speed. If you stay on schedule for heading to Costa Rica early next week, call me before you guys go in the bush," Will said as he shook hands good-bye.

Alan and Rene flew back that afternoon to Miami, with Rene continuing on to Haiti.

Alan called Eddie, his ex-recon sniper in 'Nam, on the VHF radio on the *Anne Bonny* when he got back to the marina. The two had served together in the Marine Reconnaissance Third Battalion, for one and a half tours, starting in 1969. Besides endless operations behind enemy lines, they took R and R together and had remained close friends. Alan had used Eddie—whose 'Nam nickname was "Fast Eddie"—as an outside contractor on an elimination mission last year. Fast Eddie was a first mate on an '86 Palmer and Johnson luxury yacht, based in Fort Lauderdale, which was owned by a billionaire. The billionaire had hired Fast Eddie for his excellent seamanship—and, more importantly, for his past military background—in the belief that Eddie would provide significant security for the vessel. Alan gave Eddie the pay-telephone number at the end of the dock and asked him to call in thirty minutes.

The telephone rang right on schedule. "Eddie, how are you doing?"

"I am doing great. What's up?"

"Do you have time for a consulting job starting Monday for two to three weeks?"

"Damn right. Whatever it is, I wouldn't miss it. The owner won't be back on board for two months," Eddie quickly replied.

"Can you still pull off one of those thousand-yard shots?"

"With no wind, absolutely."

"What sniper rifle do you want me to have sent down to Costa Rica?"

"Damn, love Costa Rica. Can you ship my rifle from the yacht? The yacht owner bought me the best money could buy. I am dialed in with it."

"No problem. I will send someone by the yacht tomorrow to pick it up. Are you guys still docked a pier sixty-six?"

"Yep."

"Okay, someone will pick it up tomorrow, and it will be in Costa Rica next week when we get there. He will also drop off your ticket. I negotiated your fee—twenty thousand for two weeks and thirty thousand for three weeks. Sure beats combat pay."

"Awesome, Alan. You are the best. See you next week. Looking forward to working with you again."

# CHAPTER 11

## GEARING UP IN COSTA RICA

Alan and Rene flew to Costa Rica together out of Miami. Ed dropped them off at a safe house, where all the gear was stored. He went back to the airport and picked up Eddie an hour later and dropped him off at the safe house.

Eddie was a six foot, 180-pounder on the slim side but hard as a rail. His sandy-blond hair was shaggy over his ears. He had the look of a surfer dude.

"Fast Eddie. Great to see you."

"Excellent to be back with you and Rene after last year. Is this our team?"

"We got one more man coming—Wild Bill," Alan said with a big smile.

"Wild fucking Wild Bill from 'Nam?" Eddie replied in disbelief.

"The same."

"Rene, you won't believe this guy. He always wanted to walk point. Wouldn't walk rear guard—called it the too-fucking-late guard. He was our breach and demolition guy. Totally very dangerous animal," Eddie said with a chuckle. "Alan, remember Wild Bill's sawed-off shotgun?"

"How could I ever forget?"

"Rene, did Alan tell you about the time in 'Nam where he was demoted, put in the brig, and repromoted in four hours?"

"No, he didn't. Got to hear that one."

"We will do it over drinks tonight when Wild Bill gets here," Alan replied with a chuckle.

Wild Bill arrived two hours later. He dropped his bag and gave Alan and Eddie a fist bump, pulling his open hand back like an explosion, and crisply saluted before giving both Alan and Eddie a hug.

Wild Bill was a solid six two and weighed in at 230 pounds. He was in top shape and was in the weight room several times a week. His brown hair was still in a close-cropped military style.

"Ghost, I can't believe I am with you and Eddie again. I was very surprised when the station chief in El Salvador pulled me in to tell me where I was going."

They inspected and verified all their gear, before settling in and planning to take it easy tonight and finalize the final planning review in the morning.

Eddie broke out the bottle of Bunnahabhain twenty-five-year-old single malt Scotch and the Montecristo Cuban cigars, and they sat in the living room while Bill caught up with Eddie and Alan. They were on their third drink, when Rene asked about Alan's trip to the brig and demotion story Eddie had mentioned.

"Wild Bill, do you remember the day Ghost got demoted, thrown in the brig, and repromoted in four hours?" Eddie asked with a big grin.

"Damn right I do."

"Ghost, tell Rene the story," Eddie said, not able to keep from laughing.

"No, I will leave it to you; you tell it so much better." Alan chuckled and toasted Eddie with his glass.

"I would love to. Rene, we were on a long-range recon and had been cut off twice from our planned LZs on the run by a company of crack NVA regulars for five days, thirty klicks outside the wire. We got almost no sleep and came very close to running out of ammo. We were finally picked up from a last-minute jungle emergency LZ, dangling from a fucking rope ladder, and brought back to the base. A marine major, in starched pressed khakis, walked over to us. We had never seen him before." Eddie paused for effect.

"Wild Bill had his sawed-off shotgun hanging from his belt on a lanyard. The major asked Wild Bill what type of ammo he was using in the sawed-off shotgun. Wild Bill immediately responded, 'Triple-aught lead, sir,'" Eddie said, unable to keep a straight face.

"Wild Bill, what did the major tell you?" Eddie asked, leading Bill on.

"He told me, 'Marine, the use of that ammo is against the Geneva convention.'"

"No shit?" Rene could not help saying in disbelief.

"No shit. Ghost then stripped off his field pack, still holding his folding-stock M-14 with the safety off, and walked directly over in front of the major. Our recon team went dead silent; we all held our breath. We still had full camo grease on our faces and hands. We had small pieces of bush in our boonie hats' rim holders—right out of the fucking deep bush. Tell Rene what you said, Ghost." Eddie, standing in the middle of the room, was now in full swing and on a roll.

"Fast Eddie, you are doing too good a job," Alan replied, again tipping his glass to Eddie.

"Ghost tells this major, 'Well, Major, we haven't met anyone out there yet from fucking Geneva,'" Eddie said as he doubled over laughing. Rene burst out laughing and clapped his hands. "The major stormed away in a giant huff. Ten minutes later when we are moving our gear over to our tent area, the major shows up with two MPs. The MPs hauled Alan to the brig, and we heard Alan had been demoted. They didn't even let him wipe off his camo grease. That lasted four hours. The base commander found out and blew a gasket; Alan was immediately let out of the brig and was still a captain. Can't make this shit up. We never saw that fucking major again." Eddie finished laughing so hard that he had tears running down his checks. Rene could not stop laughing. Bill just sat there with a big smile.

"Okay, one more round of drinks, and then let's turn in. We want to start early morning tomorrow," Alan said, putting out his cigar and not able to keep from laughing.

The next morning, they were all up at 7:30 a.m. Alan made Manhattan omelets using a recipe from the Camellia Grill in New Orleans. They then sat down and went over the intel, including files on each Contra guy they would be eliminating, and the maps, including key areas for withdrawal or to rally, in case the team got split up. They loaded all their weapons and loaded out their backpacks.

Alan disappeared in a back room of the safe house and came out carrying a large box. "You guys have got to see these," Alan said before setting the box on the dining-room table. He opened the box and pulled out tiger-stripe camo pants, shirts, body armor, gear vests, boonie hats, and, finally, combat boots. All the gear had the same tiger-stripe jungle camo pattern. "These are the bush uniforms for the elite unit of the Costa Rican Special Forces. Awesome, and not a straight line anywhere on this stuff."

They all came over, and Alan checked the labels and started to throw them their gear.

"What happens if we actually run into the real elite Costa Rican Special Forces?" Eddie said as he held the shirt up.

"We have to make sure we don't engage them, of course. I have the magical signed document that lets us walk away without a problem. As a backup, I also have Sandinista combat fatigues in case we want to play that card," Alan replied.

"Let's hope if we run into the Costa Rican Special Forces, we have time to actually present the fucking document," Bill replied quickly.

"It is worth the risk. The Contras won't open fire on us until we engage them when we are wearing this gear, and reportedly the Costa Ricans don't have units operating in the area where we are going, to prevent possible engagement with the Contras. Rest up; we push off at twenty-one hundred hours tonight. Final gear check is at twenty hundred hours. Wear civilian clothes for the drive up; we will do final dress out and gear up before we leave the Jeep. You are on your own now until twenty hundred," Alan finished before taking his new clothing gear back to his room.

Alan called Natalie at the London CIA station when he got back to his room. In minutes, she was on the line.

"Hey, mate, hope all is well. I just wanted to let you know I will be out of touch for at least a couple of weeks, possibly three."

"Thanks for the heads-up. Take care of yourself, mate. You need to take a trip over, and we need to go back to Bordeaux. I certainly also wouldn't mind coming for another sail in the Bahamas."

"We should do both. I'll call you when I get back."

# CHAPTER 12

## LOCK AND LOAD, ROCK 'N' ROLL

*Day one*

Alan drove directly up to the Infiernillo River, on back roads for the last twenty miles, near the San Juan River, which divides Costa Rica and Nicaragua. Alan found the area he planned to pull off to camouflage the Jeep in the bush five and a half miles from the Contra encampment. He pulled the Jeep fifty yards off the road, stopping in an area surrounded by five-foot-thick bushes. Eddie got out with a machete and carefully cut a path to drive the Jeep in and still be able to pull back brush to make it disappear. They unloaded from the Jeep and used their night-vision gear to dress, gear up, apply camo grease to their faces and hands, and place small pieces of bush into their boonie hat headbands. They did a final gear check for one another, before they moved out slowly and quietly.

They silently began to move through the jungle. They were almost invisible in their camo and used hand signals only. They stopped every thirty minutes for five minutes to looking and listen. They were moving in a fire-team wedge formation, with Wild Bill on point carrying a Stoner 63 machine gun with a drum magazine holding 150 rounds. Alan was on the right flank, carrying his folding-stock M-14 and a M-72, 66-millimeter light antitank weapon (LAW). Rene, bringing up the rear, was armed with an M16 with a grenade launcher, and Eddie was on the left flank, carrying his British L-96 sniper rifle designed for the Special Air Service (SAS) and a M-72 LAW. Each team member had two ammo belts for Bill's Stoner machine gun, except Bill; he had four ammo belts. They also had C-4 explosives and claymore antipersonnel mines stowed in their backpacks. They all had three frag and three smoke grenades and their Beretta sidearm with silencers. They were four extremely dangerous men, loaded for bear.

They proceeded east-southeast for the area that had been identified by the U-2 reconnaissance aircraft. This area had no Contra patrols and was isolated from any other local villagers. No Contras or villagers were seen during their movement, and they arrived without incident. The area was perfect. It was a dry creek bed, which provided excellent natural berm protections on three of the sides. Once they had unloaded their gear, Eddie and Rene began to cut six-inch-diameter trees with their razor-sharp machetes and pile dirt using their trench shovels to build a berm on the open end of the position. Bill had gone out to scout the primary, secondary, and emergency LZs in case they needed a chopper. He reported back to the team that the LZs were found in good order. Alan used his pager to send the code back to Langley that they had arrived at the encampment area with no issues. He got back the received-and-confirmed code right away. They spent the next hour laying out gear to lighten their field packs to the bare essentials needed for a single patrol or mission. They all ate some MRE rations and drank a half quart of water. Eddie took first sentry watch. Alan, Rene, and Bill all took naps to rest for the night.

That night at eight Alan huddled with Eddie and Bill while Rene was on sentry duty. "Tonight, Eddie and I will go in for a recon on the Contra encampment, listening on the patrol assignments for the evening with our listening gear. We will also get a first look to see how effective the spray tags we did at the interviews were for the next step of planning," Alan said quietly.

"Explain to me again the tagging details," Bill interjected.

"Sure, Bill. When Rene and I were here doing our interviews, we both had small sprayers with a mist liquid that was noiseless. The mist had no smell and left no feel or sign of wetness. Rene and I had a hand sign on the personnel we identified from the file and interviews, and we would spray their boots under the interview table. They had no idea we were doing it. The mist spray is a reflector that can be sited with infrared scopes. At night, the boots will have a light-green glow on the front tips of their boots. This, of course, will allow us to easily identify our targets," Alan explained.

"Wow, that is scary stuff," Bill said in disbelief. "You are targeted and have no idea."

"I searched the ten guys I eliminated originally, and they had no infrared equipment, so they wouldn't be able see the tags themselves," Alan responded. "Our recon tonight will tell the story."

Alan and Eddie geared up and did a gear check for each other before heading out on the recon. Alan brought Eddie back to the ravine near a fallen tree that provided both excellent cover and a view overlooking the encampment. The area had no signs of anyone in the area since Alan had left. They settled in, setting up the Super Ear listening device, pulling out their FLIR scopes, and scanning the encampment.

"Damn, look there at two o'clock. Check out the green-glow boot tips," Eddie said quietly with awe.

The light-green glow could be clearly seen on the boot tips of the trooper walking through the camp. Suddenly another trooper came out of the command tent with a brighter-green glow on the tips of his boots.

"The Langley backroom techs said the spray mist wouldn't wash off in water and rain; they sure as hell were right. Looks like the commander's boots that haven't been in the bush are brighter," Alan whispered.

The troopers for the two patrols begin to gather in front of the command-tent fly, doing gear checks on each other and waiting for their briefing. Alan and Eddie could see two troopers with a light-green glow on their boot tips and the commander and the executive officer with brighter-green glow on their boot tips.

"Okay, this is going to work. I want to follow which patrol heads toward the village. We won't do anything unless they threaten the villagers or attack the women. I didn't come all the way here to have something happen to those villagers before we start action tomorrow," Alan whispered.

Alan and Eddie followed the patrols to the abandoned foot-bridge border crossing into Nicaragua and waited until they were clear of the crossing area before following over. Eddie picked up the fresh trail of the patrol heading east along the river, and within twenty minutes, they picked up the rear guard with their FLIR scopes, before flipping down the night-vision gear. The patrol moved directly to the village and passed through the village without incident. Alan and Eddie took up a position to await the return of the patrol to the village. In three hours, they picked up the point man coming into the village. The patrol again passed through without any interaction with the villagers.

Alan and Eddie waited until the patrol had cleared and then moved back, following the patrol to the bridge crossing. They again gave the patrol forty minutes to clear on the other side of the bridge, before they crossed and headed back to their encampment. A hundred yards out from their encampment, Alan gave his jungle-bird whistle, and they waited. They got back a similar whistle and proceeded into the encampment.

"Rene, you won't believe this shit. The tips of the bad guys' boots have a green glow. Best individual target indicators I have ever seen," Eddie excitedly said as he stripped off his gear.

Al Dugan

"Excellent. We got to tip our hats to the backroom planning and tech guys. This will definitely help eliminate collateral damage. We also know we are done when we don't see any more glowing-green boot tips; we will know then we have eliminated all the bad guys. This is looking like another Picasso," Rene responded immediately.

"We don't want to get ahead of ourselves here. We got a lot of work to do to finish this right. The tags are a great first start. I will take the next sentry shift after I eat. We will lie low tomorrow and be ready for tomorrow night. Rene, give Bill a brief when he comes off sentry." Alan finished his MRE rations and drank his half quart of water and picked up his M-14 and moved out to the sentry position to take over from Bill.

*Day two*
Shortly after sunset, Eddie and Rene began to gear up. Eddie was checking his sniper sight on the L-96 sniper rifle. Alan and Rene reviewed the map and discussed the different sniper locations on the Nicaraguan side of the San Juan River. They picked out three areas and called Eddie over to take a look. Eddie liked all three options. At 7:00 p.m., Eddie and Rene headed out to pick the sniper-position option they would use and to set up. Alan and Bill also geared up to take up the surveillance position over the Contra encampment.

At 9:30 p.m., the Contra troopers began to gear up and head for their briefing at the command-tent fly. There were two troopers going on patrols who had the green glow of their boot tips, as well as the commander and executive officer. The briefing took thirty minutes, before the two patrols headed out of the encampment toward the footbridge with the abandoned Immigration and Customs hut. Alan called Rene on their headgear radio set, which operated on a unique frequency that could not be picked up by the Contra radios.

74

"We have two patrols proceeding to the footbridge. We have two target troopers in the first patrol. Both patrols are moving in fire-team columns. The targets are in the first column; both men on the left flank of the column are in the one and two positions. Over," Alan whispered.

"Roger that. We are set up in the option-two position—excellent sight lines. Eddie is ready. Over."

"Roger that. We await your results. Over."

Rene and Eddie picked up the first patrol with their FLIR scopes on the Costa Rica side of the river. The patrol slowly crossed the bridge, closing their formation until they exited the bridge and then again spread to a fire-team column. The two targeted troopers could be easily seen again on the left flank of the column in the option-one and option-two positions. Rene was acting as the spotter and relayed the info to Eddie.

"I got the first guy. Ready to fire in thirty seconds," Eddie whispered back.

"You have a green light."

"Roger that."

The L-96 sniper rifle whispered, and Rene watched the column carefully. The trooper in the option-one position dropped in his tracks. He didn't move after he went down. The shot was six hundred yards, so the silenced shot was not heard by the troopers. The second targeted trooper in the option-two position moved up to see what had happened to the patrol leader ahead of him. He leaned down and rolled over the patrol leader and immediately noted the wound.

The second targeted trooper stood back up and yelled "Sniper" at the exact moment the round hit him in the head—perfect shot. The rest of the troopers dropped flat to the ground, covering all sides with their weapons. Rene could see the radioman talking, probably with the second patrol and then HQ. Alan and Bill spotted the commander and executive officer follow a trooper on a full run back to the command-tent fly. Activity began to pick up all over the Contra encampment.

"We have two targets eliminated. Over," Rene whispered over the radio headset.

"They have reported back to HQ. We have activity back here. Over," Alan whispered in the headset.

"The second patrol has taken up a position on the other side of the bridge. The troopers in the first patrol are prone, not moving now. We plan to sit tight unless we have significant troop movement in our direction. It doesn't look like they know where the shots came from. If we do withdraw, we will pull back to rally point three. Over," Rene finished as he continued to carefully sweep both sides of the river for any movement.

"We have a new patrol gearing up at the HQ. We have two targets in this patrol. Looks like we are going to get an unexpected bonus round. Over," Alan responded.

The first patrol that had crossed the bridge began to crouch, moving off to the east, away from Rene and Eddie. The second patrol crossed the bridge, taking cover on the bridge on the way over. They quickly deployed and moved low, due north, once over the bridge in a fire-team column.

"The first patrol headed east, and the second patrol headed north. I expect the new patrol will head west toward us. We will eliminate the two targets in that patrol before we withdraw to rally point three. Over," Rene advised.

In an hour, the third patrol appeared on the Costa Rica side of the bridge and began to move across, taking cover. The first man off the bridge had the green-glow boot-tip target marker, and Rene tapped Eddie, confirming that he take the shot. The targeted trooper began to move in a crouch forward for the jungle trail to the west toward Rene and Eddie. The L-96 sniper rifle whispered, and the trooper dropped in his tracks. The troopers on the bridge took up defense positions and began to withdraw slowly back to the Costa Rica side of the river.

Once they were on that side, Rene, using his scope, and Eddie, using the sniper sight, swept the troops. They both picked up the green-boot target marker on one of the troopers leading the discussion with the huddled patrol.

"Can you get him? Eight hundred and thirty-six yards," Rene said quietly.

"Piece of cake," Eddie whispered back. Thirty seconds later, the L-96 sniper rifle whispered. Rene carefully watched as the targeted trooper dropped. Two of the troopers grabbed his arms, dragging him back to the nearby jungle, while the remaining troopers followed.

"We have eliminated both targets in patrol number three. The patrol dragged the last target into the jungle and retreated. Over."

"Well done, guys. We have no more activity gearing up at the HQ. The command-tent fly is buzzing, and we are listening. They have no idea what is going on and keep referring to another Sandinista sniper. They plan to pull all the patrols back. The other two patrols will be back at the bridge shortly. Over," Alan whispered back over the headset.

"Roger that. We will hold our position until they return and cross the bridge. Over," Rene reported back. He turned and slapped Eddie on the back. "Damn fine shooting, my man. I now understand why you were Alan's man in 'Nam."

"Thanks, bud. Much appreciated. No wind was a big help. I will have to buy the backroom tech guys a drink. Those target locators were fucking brilliant."

Rene and Eddie waited a full hour after the last Contra patrol entered the jungle on the Costa Rica side, before heading back to their encampment. Alan and Bill continued to listen to the discussions and planning at the Contra HQ, until the commander wrapped up the meetings at 6:00 a.m. Alan and Bill slowly and quietly backed out of their surveillance position and headed back to their encampment.

When they got to the encampment, Rene was on sentry duty, and Eddie was sleeping with a poncho pulled over his head. Alan and Bill sat down and immediately ate MREs and drank a half quart of water. Both then went to their sleeping gear and pulled their ponchos over their heads and slept until Rene came in to wake Eddie up for sentry duty. Both Bill and Alan sat up; Rene sat down and fixed coffee using their small Sterno burner.

"Damn, Alan—Eddie can shoot. Those were some awesome shots. The eight-hundred-and-thirty-six-yard shot over the river was amazing," Rene said as he handed Alan and Bill coffee.

"You don't know…Eddie pulled off a nineteen-hundred-yard shot in 'Nam in a light breeze. Took out an NVA battalion commander in his own HQ. I was his spotter. Eddie is magic. The NVA put a bounty on both Eddie and me after that shot—fifty thousand US dollars. That would have been a whole junk full of dong dollars," Alan said with a chuckle after taking a sip of coffee. "I will brief you and Eddie when he comes in off sentry. Bill listened in with me, and he is already fully up to speed. The really good news is they think they have another Sandinista sniper, just as the backroom boys had planned. The cover is working well."

After Bill relieved Eddie on sentry, Eddie sat down with Rene and Alan and ate his MREs while Alan provided the brief.

"Well, we have today and tonight to rest. Their next action and patrols are planned for tomorrow night. They are going sniper hunting. Apparently, the last Sandinista sniper got three of their troopers before they hunted him down. Turned out he was a seventeen-year-old Nicaraguan boy when they finally tracked him down and killed him," Alan said with a pause, waiting for any questions or comments. Both Rene and Eddie just nodded.

"Their plan for tomorrow night is the use of boats crossing to the west and east of the footbridge to trap the sniper between the two patrols as they close on the bridge. The good news is they believe the shots were not more than four hundred and fifty yards, and the shooter had been close enough to the river to make the cross-river shot. They are very concerned the sniper has a silencer. Of course, the kid didn't have one. They have decided that this sniper is a pro and has a spotter—a real Sandinista sniper team."

"Well, that is great news," Eddie interjected.

"Agreed. The cover is holding up better than I hoped. We did hear the names of the two patrol leaders for tomorrow night; both are targets. What was a surprise was the executive officer is going out with the patrol to the west," Alan said and leaned back and stretched.

"Do we take him out or wait until the end?" Rene asked the question they were all considering.

"I want to think it over today, but my first thought is we don't take him out. I don't want a new executive officer until we are done, and Ed, their CIA liaison, can come in and build from the top down clean. Your thoughts?"

"I agree," Rene immediately responded.

"Piece of cake. Let's save him and the commander for last, as originally planned," Eddie chimed in.

Alan worked the rest of the afternoon on the action plan for the next night. When he was finished, he reviewed it with each team member individually to make sure he got each person's input. When they had finished the planning reviews and they had full agreement, it was time to relax, until it was their turn on sentry watch.

### Day three

The next day was quiet, and they began midday preparing for the mission that night. They all cleaned their weapons and rechecked their gear and loaded out their backpacks with more ammo. Alan and Bill each loaded C-4s and two claymores into their backpacks.

At sunset, they set out for the footbridge. Alan and Eddie waited for Bill and Rene, while they went in to take a quick final look at the Contra encampment before the action tonight. All was found normal; the Contras were just getting ready to gear up for tonight. When Bill and Rene came back, they all proceeded to the bridge and took up positions on the Costa Rica side to assure the crossing was safe. After thirty minutes, they did a quick low-crouch full run across the bridge and entered the jungle on the Nicaragua side of the San Juan River.

After waiting for fifteen minutes covering the bridge, they split up into two groups: Alan and Eddie proceeded west, and Bill and Rene east to the designated landing spots for the Contra boats they picked up when listening in on the Contra planning. Each boat was to land one mile, both east and west, of the footbridge on the Nicaragua bank of the San Juan River. The Contras then planned to sweep from each side toward the bridge to trap the sniper team.

Alan and Eddie, as well as Rene and Bill, set up four hundred yards in raised protected locations at the expected boat landings on both the east and west side with a perfect line of sight of the landing area. Both landing areas had fifty yards or more of open space before the jungle cover. They were perfect places for ambushes. Both boats came ashore very near the planned ambush locations. The Contras at both locations took their time unloading, exposing their troopers, and allowing easy ID of the targeted Contras with the green glow on their boot tips.

At the west ambush site, the brighter-green boot tips of the executive officer could be clearly distinguished from the other two targeted troopers. The Contra troopers organized into the typical fire-team column. Alan and Eddie quickly picked off the two troopers with the target markers and pinned down the rest of the patrol in the clearing area. They went to full automatic and laid down a large amount of fire. The Contra trooper executive officer ordered a retreat to the boat. They loaded quickly and pushed off, heading back to the Costa Rica bank of the river.

The Contras who landed to the east also formed a fire-team column, and Rene immediately picked off the targeted patrol leader. Bill, who was at a closer position to provide cross fire, opened up with his Stoner 63 machine gun, cutting down the second target, who was the NCO. The Contra troopers were now completely disorganized without their patrol leader and their NCO. The Contra troops began to get up and run back to the boat in complete disorder. Bill kept the automatic fire up, just shooting high over their heads. Finally, they all got aboard the boat and pushed off for the Costa Rica bank of the river.

"Damn, those were some sorry excuses for soldiers," Bill finally said after they ceased fire.

"Team One, our mission is complete. Over," Eddie radioed to Alan on the headset.

"Roger that; mission is complete here as well. Rally back at the footbridge, north side. Over," Alan replied before he and Bill moved out. They met up and carefully and quickly crossed the bridge and went back to their encampment.

At the encampment, they took off their gear and sat down and ate MREs and drank water. Eddie grabbed his MREs and water and went out to the sentry position, taking first watch.

"Like shooting fish in a barrel," Rene finally said.

"No shit. You should have seen the Chinese fire drill of the retreat at our end," Bill added.

"Roger that. Okay, we are down to the commander, XO, and the sergeant major," Alan said before pulling out the map. After a half hour, he leaned back. "Well, we can do it either way: go in get them or we can let Eddie pick them off. I do want to go back tonight and see what the security looks like now around the tent area for the commander, XO, and the sergeant major. I will take

Eddie, as he can also look at the possibility of just the sniper-shoot option. Your thoughts?"

"Your call, boss. I am good either way," Rene replied.

"Same here, Ghost," Bill chimed in.

"Roger that," Alan said, before walking over and picking up his poncho and lying down on his sleeping bedroll and pulling the poncho over his head.

"Damn, Ghost, you can sleep anywhere," Bill said with a chuckle, before picking up his Stoner to go relieve Eddie, who would be going out tonight.

At sunset Alan and Eddie headed for the Contra encampment to their surveillance position. They carefully examined the area with their FLIR scopes, before moving in and setting up the Super Ear listening device. There was significant activity going on in and around the command-tent fly. They started to pick up what sounded like the final wrap-up of a major mission briefing, where the commander was taking questions.

"Are we sure there are only four of them? They hit us really hard when we used the boats," they heard a voice ask.

"Reportedly, there are only four, but they are top-notch, very dangerous assassins," someone responded.

"You said our operation is a kill mission. What if they do try to surrender?" another voice asked.

"This is a no-prisoners action. I understand there is very little chance of any of them surrendering." This time Alan knew it was the commander speaking. "We gear up in four hours. They are camped somewhere south of here. The two companies will begin to sweep south a klick from here until we find them."

The commander then advised one of the company captains would also be in charge of the entire operation.

Alan and Eddie looked at each other, before Alan radioed back to Rene. "We have been set up, and our cover is blown. You are going to have two companies that will be approaching on your encampment sweeping from north in approximately four to five hours. Please confirm. Over."

"Roger that, Ghost. Confirm cover broken, and two companies will be sweeping in from the north in four to five hours for ambush at our encampment. Over," Rene came back over the headset.

"Looks like the commander, XO, and sergeant major are going to remain in their encampment. We plan to stay here and take them out. I want you and Bill to pack up and head back to the Jeep as soon as possible. Eddie and I will meet you there when we are done. Over," Alan whispered quietly.

"Roger that. I will let you know as soon as we start to move out. Ghost, if you and Eddie need help, we will come. Do you want me to set the claymores? Over," Rene replied with concern.

"No. Only use the claymores to get away or defend yourselves. At that point minimize-collateral-damage protocol ends. We will advise as soon as our mission is complete, and we are on the move. Over," Alan whispered.

Thirty minutes later Rene radioed, "We are moving out now. Over."

Alan and Eddie sat quietly, trying to absorb and understand how their cover had been blown. Finally, Alan spoke first. "I know it wasn't Ed," he whispered quietly.

"I agree," Eddie whispered back. "My Spanish could be better, but I understood enough of what they said to scare the shit out of me."

"They know there are four of us, we are very dangerous, and we're camped to the south. How the fuck could they have gotten that? Until now, they believed they were looking for a Sandinista two-man sniper team," Alan whispered, not able to keep the anger out of his voice.

"Thank God they don't know everything—most importantly our ability to hear everything they are saying."

"Okay, let's eliminate these last three guys, and we will deal with the leak when we get back. We will do whatever we need to extract. No rules."

"You can bet your ass on that, Ghost."

Alan and Eddie watched as the two companies began to gear up and organize. The commander, executive officer, and sergeant major provided a final brief, confirming the basics of the mission, before the companies began to move out as scheduled.

"We have companies on the move. Estimated ETA at our encampment in two hours. Over," Alan radioed to Rene.

"Roger that. We are well clear now. We have left a clear indication of our encampment. Bill and I have also beaten a new path east away from the encampment to give them a rabbit hole to follow. Over."

"Roger that. Over."

Eddie moved farther down the ridge and to the left of Alan's position to get clean shots into the command-tent fly area. The commander, executive officer, and sergeant major were drinking coffee, looking at the map, and discussing the assassins that had been sent to disrupt their operation.

"I have a perfect shot on all three now, no matter how they take cover or run. Over," Eddie whispered over the headset.

"You have a green light to shoot when ready. Over."

In a minute Alan saw the executive officer drop to the ground, without a sound. The sergeant major rushed over to see what had happened. As he rolled over, the executive officer fell over on top of him. The commander took off running into the camp, screaming, "The assassins are here, the assassins...", before he dropped in his tracks.

"Moving back to you. Over," Eddie whispered.

The camp was a mass of confusion as troopers ran over to the commander and into the tent fly. Eddie reached Alan, and they began to withdraw to the Jeep. They moved thirty minutes at a time, stopping and carefully making sure they were not being followed. Alan and Eddie were able to move through the jungle, leaving a trail only the very best of trackers could find.

Four hours later Alan and Eddie were approaching the Jeep. Alan gave his jungle-bird whistle, and he and Eddie crouched perfectly still, weapons ready. The response whistle came back immediately. Alan and Eddie proceeded to the Jeep. All four men stripped off their clothes, wiped off the camo grease, changed into civilian clothes, and drove away. They all sat quietly, not saying a word for over an hour.

"So what the fuck was that about, Ghost?" Eddie finally said. "They knew our unit size and our fucking location."

"Well, they didn't know everything, or we would probably all be dead. I will find out who blew our cover and why. You can bet the farm on it," Alan said in a steel-cold voice.

"Are we going to be safe back at the last safe house?" Bill said quietly.

"I will call Ed when we are a half hour out, and I will arrange a meeting outside that safe house. I have the same concern. I would expect it is safe, but I am not taking anything for granted now. I do trust Ed," Alan replied, not able to keep the anger out of his voice.

When they were thirty minutes outside San Jose, Alan stopped and called Ed from a pay telephone. He picked up right away. "We need to meet—another location than the last safe house."

"Are you guys okay? What happened?"

"We are all fine. The mission is complete. Our cover was blown yesterday, and the Contras sent two companies to go after us. Let's meet, and I will go over the details."

"Roger that. Meet me at this new safe-house address. I will send it to you on your pager."

"No, give me the address now. I am not using the pager until we talk," Alan quickly replied as Ed gave him the address.

They pulled up to the block where the new safe house was located, and Alan pulled over. Both Rene and Eddie, with their Berettas in shoulder holsters under their windbreakers, got out of the Jeep. They walked down toward the house and were gone a few minutes, before Eddie stepped out to the sidewalk and waved them to come. Alan pulled into the driveway, and Rene waved him into the garage and closed the garage door.

Ed was waiting with Eddie in the living room as they came in the house. "Damn glad to see you guys. Tell me what happened."

"I will give you the Cliff Notes version. Everything went as planned until last night. We were eliminating the select targets as they patrolled. The night before, all the targets but the commander, XO, and sergeant major were eliminated. Eddie and I went to surveil and decide how we would take out these last three. Right when we arrived, they were preparing for a large two-company operation and were conducting the final brief. They were coming after us. We listened in on the end of the questions with our Super Ear. It was clearly stated there were four of us, we were dangerous assassins, and we were camped south of their HQ. Before this meeting, they had only talked about finding a Sandinista two-man sniper team," Alan explained, clearly angry, and sat back and waited for anyone else to comment.

Ed sat very still, not saying a word for several minutes. Alan, Rene, Bill, and Eddie sat waiting for him to say something. "Guys, I have no idea how they got the intel. My two reports only went back to the top guy in operations," he finally responded. It was apparent Ed had no idea where the leak came from. He sat quietly, and it was obvious he was running every possible source in his head. "I just don't see how they got the intel."

"Well, now we have a real mystery. Is there any way your reporting got intercepted without you knowing it?" Alan carefully asked to show his confidence in Ed.

"No. I sent two reports on your mission to the top guy only, using the encrypted data line. I would find it hard to believe it has been compromised, but we will, of course, have to investigate this as a breach of mission data at our San Juan station."

"Well, the good news is that the mission was one hundred percent successful eliminating targets, and there was no other collateral damage. You have a battalion waiting and in need of new leadership," Rene replied to Ed to take the pressure off the leak discussion.

"Can you have your logistics person book us out tomorrow? Rene will be going directly back to Port-au-Prince through Miami. Bill can go back directly to El Salvador, and Eddie and I will be going back to Miami. Also need to have my M-14 sent to company logistics and Eddie's L-96 delivered back to him in Miami. I want to thank you for all your help, and we, of course, trust you one hundred percent; we want to make sure that is clear," Alan said quietly.

"Thanks, guys. I am deeply disturbed. Thank God you guys all made it out clean. We will get to the bottom of the leaked intel if it was from down here. That is a promise. Your half bottle of single malt is over on the bar top. I want to head back to the station and set up your flights and start the leak investigation," Ed said, before shaking hands with them all before he left.

Eddie went to the bar and threw everyone a Cuban cigar and poured four neat drinks of the single malt. "Cheers, guys," he said as they gave one another a fist bump and pulled back their open hands back like an explosion before they crisply saluted. They finished the bottle of single malt and the cigars, unwinding before they turned in.

The flights back the next day went smoothly, right on time. Alan, Rene, and Eddie were in first class, and Alan finished his post-action report and sent it by FedEx at the Miami Airport to Langley when they landed.

# CHAPTER 13

## R AND R UNWIND

Alan called Natalie as soon as he got back to the *Anne Bonny*. "Hello, mate. How are you?"

"Wow, you are back early. So glad to hear from you."

"We finished up early. Can you come over for a sail first? There could be some loose ends on this last one, and I better lie close."

"Oh really, mate. Twist my arm to leave dreary London and go sailing in the Bahamas with you?"

"Great. How do you look, timing wise?"

"Let me check, but definitely this week. I just got back myself from a quick job."

"Page me your flight and arrival date. I will be at the gate, mate."

The next day was a light rain, and all was quiet. Alan sat and read a book under the cockpit canopy. He received a page with the date and flight; Natalie would be there in two days.

The following day Alan worked around the boat, getting it ready for the sail with Natalie. It was a beautiful, sunny day with a light wind rattling the rigging. Alan had just finished washing down the teak deck, when his pager went off from Langley. Alan walked down to the pay telephone and called Will. "Hey, Will, you paged?"

"Yes, I just finished reviewing your post-action report. I was absolutely shocked." Will paused, waiting for Alan to comment.

"You think you were shocked…any word on the leak?"

"No, we are still reviewing, and Ed down in Costa Rica is turning the place upside down. He is plenty pissed off, but so far everything down there looks clean."

"Ed told me he only sent his updates encrypted to the top guy in operations. It can't be Langley, can it?"

"We are checking everything. Nothing is sacred. This was as highly classified a mission as they come, not to mention the extreme danger that was involved for you and your team. I will keep you advised. Fine job by you guys down there. Results don't get any better than that—one hundred percent target elimination, and no collateral damage despite the leak. You guys showed excellent restraint."

"Needless to say, let me know as soon as you find the leak. FYI, I have Natalie arriving tomorrow for a week of sailing, unless either one of us gets a code red."

"Excellent. You are a lucky dog. You enjoy, and I will page you if we discover anything on the leak."

Alan picked up Natalie at the airport the next day, and they were under way shortly after they got on board. Natalie changed and came out in a bikini top and shorts, carrying two Red Stripes.

"I am so damn pale. I look like a ghost."

"You have that English beautiful porcelain look," Alan said with a chuckle, before Natalie swatted him on his arm.

"Don't want to talk shop, but I was back at the Grand Hotel and Bordeaux and sure was missing you, mate. Used my clothes from our mission last year when we were there. Thought you would enjoy that the concierge remembered me and asked me to pass on his best regards to you."

"That is your problem—you are too stunning and beautiful. Men never forget you. Hope it didn't cause an issue on the assignment."

"No, it was no problem. I was meeting people outside the hotel and just had to have the Grand to show I was a high roller. I was buying stolen art. The proceeds are being used to fund some Central American enemy black ops. We have advised Langley of the Central America connection."

"Okay. Enough shoptalk. Come steer this yacht, and let me see how well you have kept your touch."

The rest of the week was simply outstanding: sailing, swimming, diving, windsurfing, and dancing. The weather was perfect the entire week, with a steady fifteen-knot trade wind. Alan and Natalie now were so absolutely comfortable together. The sex was often, athletic, and world-class.

The last day they had sailed back to North Andros and anchored for the day. That evening they sat in the cockpit, sipping the Dark and Stormy drinks Alan had just made. Alan heard his pager vibrating below. He ducked down to the navigation station, where he had left his pager. It was Langley but not urgent.

"Alan, I have enjoyed this so much. Thank you. Is that another assignment?"

"Right now just a call in—not urgent. I will call after we dock tomorrow. Right now I just want to enjoy the views, all of them," he said with a big smile. Natalie came over and grabbed his glass and pulled him down below.

The next afternoon they docked. Natalie was leaving the next day on an early flight. Alan made sure the *Anne Bonny* was all fast, before jumping down to use the pay telephone on the dock.

"Will, wanted to get back to you. We just docked at Dinner Key."

"Hope you guys had fun; I don't doubt that. I wanted to give you an update on the leak. We are now sure it was not Costa Rica. That is airtight. Ed asked us to let you know this as soon as we could. We are baffled on how the leak occurred. We have four Langley folks in the lie-detector room today. I will keep you advised."

"Will, was Colonel West informed about our operation?"

Will was silent for a short time. "No, he shouldn't have been. Why did you ask?"

"Ed has such bad vibes about the guy that it just seemed like a question that should be asked."

"Be careful with that one, Alan. It is a serious charge to even mention the colonel may be involved in putting agents in harm's way."

"Okay. Let me know when you get to the bottom. How is Ed doing with restaffing the battalion?"

"Don't know. I will have to ask him. I will let you know."

That night Alan took Natalie to Ruth's Chris Steakhouse for the final dinner. They started with BBQ shrimp and champagne. They finished it off with a great bottle of French Bordeaux and the large fillets with baked potatoes.

"Well, mate, are you trying to get me drunk? You know it really isn't necessary...we never see steaks like that in London," Natalie said before leaning over and kissing Alan. "Thank you so much for the sailing trip, and this final dinner was just perfect."

"Let me make sure this last assignment is cleaned up, and I will definitely come over the pond, and we will go back to the Grand Hotel in Bordeaux. That's a promise."

The rest of the night was perfect as well. The next morning, Alan drove her to the airport and walked her to the gate. They called boarding, and Alan walked her over.

"Safe trip back, mate."

"Thank you again. I had a wonderful time. I actually got some sun. I will miss you, mate," Natalie said as she wrapped herself around Alan and gave him a deep kiss. Alan watched as she boarded the aircraft. At that moment, his pager went off.

"Will, your timing is impeccable. Natalie just boarded for her trip home. What's up?"

"Are you ready for your first Asia Pacific assignment?"

"Roger that. Are you sending a package?"

"You will have it tomorrow. Look it over, and call me after you finish your review. This will be quite a challenge for your first assignment in a new region, but I have no doubt you can handle it. Oh, by the way, you will have a partner for the language issue and the lay of the land. You get a new wife…"

"Roger that. Another new wife? You guys are killing me with future alimony," Alan said with a chuckle. "Any word on the leak?"

"No. The four who took lie detectors all passed. We are really at a loss for how this happened. The very top guy is not happy. But you can bet the farm we will find the leak."

The package came the next day, delivered directly to the *Anne Bonny*. Alan spent the next four hours reviewing all the info in the thick file. He put everything away in the false door cabinet, where he stored his weapons and gear, and walked down to the pay telephone.

"Will here."

"Just finished reviewing the package. Wow."

"I figured that would be your first comment."

"Okay, let's clear the elephant in the room. You are asking me to fly into Taipei and hunt down and eliminate two North Koreans trying to eliminate a visiting US Marine general. Why wouldn't this issue be handled by the general's security unit or the Taiwanese special police?"

"Very simple. They would have to apprehend them, and the North Koreans would then be sent back to North Korea. We want to send a message: you try this, and you die."

"Okay. That is what I expected. After I eliminate these two guys, you then want me to fly to Hong Kong and eliminate a North Korean colonel there on official business?"

"Yes. We want them to know we won't stand by after they try to pull off this type of operation. If you don't have a proper window, you, of course, can call off the assignment. Your partner speaks Mandarin, Cantonese, and Korean and knows the lay of the land in both operating areas. You read her background, experience, and expertise?"

"Sure. She looks like she will be perfect. No problem with her. Okay, I will handle the two North Koreans, and we will give the second part of the mission our best shot. My cover into Hong Kong is interesting."

"Yes, it was an easy fit. The entire week you will be there for a conference on offshore oil production and logistics. You have the perfect experience from your work running supply vessels in the oil patch in the Gulf of Mexico. You will be working for a CIA shell company that provides oil-patch logistics consulting services."

# CHAPTER 14

## TAIPEI

Alan flew business class out the next day to Los Angeles on American Airlines, connecting with Cathay Pacific nonstop to Taipei. He took the blue pill issued by the Company for international travel and slept almost the entire thirteen-hour flight. He had a carry-on bag and was first to Immigration and Customs and cleared quickly. As he exited customs, he saw right away the incredibly beautiful Chinese woman holding a sign with "Talbot," his cover name. She was a slim five foot eight but well-built and obviously athletic. She had long black hair to her waist and light-brown eyes with touches of green.

Alan made eye contact, and she walked to the end of the rail to meet him. "Welcome to Taiwan, Mr. Talbot. The car is parked close by." They quietly walked out to the short-time parking area, and she led Alan over to a black Mercedes E Class AMG and popped the trunk. Alan dropped in his bag and got in on the passenger side.

"Do you want to use aliases now?" she asked in perfect English.

"Yes, Lynn, let's start right away. Do you like Sue?"

"Will do, Blake. Sue is fine. You have quite a reputation. I hear your nickname is 'Legend.' I am looking forward to working with you."

"Well, I read your background, experience, and expertise, so the feeling is mutual. You speak perfect English?"

"My mom was American; my Chinese dad spoke Mandarin. I majored in languages at Stanford, where I learned Korean and Cantonese. Your Beretta is in the side-door pocket. It has a loaded magazine but no round in the chamber. All the rest of our gear is at the safe house, where we are going now."

The safe house was in the hills above Taipei in the Wenshan District, nestled in the beautiful green mountains. When they arrived, Alan immediately examined the gear he had ordered, which was still loaded in a large duffel. Everything had been supplied.

"How about dinner? There is a great restaurant near here that has excellent fresh seafood," Lynn asked.

"Sounds great."

Seafood at the restaurant was excellent: fresh fish and crab. They had a bottle of French Chardonnay before heading back to the safe house.

"The two Koreans should be arriving tomorrow night. We have twenty-four/seven surveillance at the airport to pick them up as soon as they land. We know they will be flying in from Hong Kong. Our man on the inside in North Korea has kept our surveillance team advised on a real-time basis. The surveillance team will follow the North Koreans to where they are staying. Intel indicates they will be at the Grand Hotel of Taipei, a high-end hotel landmark," she said, pausing to allow Alan to comment.

"Excellent. You and the team have done a superb job setting this one up. I will see you in the morning. I plan to take a two-mile run before breakfast."

"Great. I will run with you. See you in the morning."

Alan awoke at 6:00 a.m., still adjusting to the twelve-hour time change but felt better than he expected. He dressed in shorts and a T-shirt and slipped on his running shoes. Lynn was already waiting, drinking a cup of tea in the kitchen. She was wearing a sleeveless T-shirt and black leggings and looked simply amazing and extremely athletic. "Want a cup of tea?"

"That would be great."

Alan finished the tea, and they went for a two-mile run through the rolling, green hills. The air was fresh and clean and still cool in the early-morning hours. Lynn was a real athlete and kept up stride for stride with Alan, including a full sprint the last quarter of a mile.

They ate a breakfast of fresh fruit and scrambled eggs and bacon and reviewed the planned action. Lynn had the key details down pat. Alan felt ready when they finished.

"That is quite a car you have out there."

"Yes, it is a real thoroughbred," Lynn said. "I have taken offensive and defensive driving courses in it. It is simply amazing."

"Great. Let's hope you don't have to prove it tomorrow."

They spent a few hours relaxing and chatting. Alan finally went back to his room until dinner. Alan barbecued steaks for their dinner in the early evening. During dinner, the telephone rang, and Lynn answered. She spoke in Mandarin Chinese. Alan could pick up the dialect but didn't understand a word. After a few minutes, she hung up. "The North Korean hit team has just cleared customs. They were picked up by a car from the Grand Hotel, so everything looks like what was expected in the intel. The marine general arrives in two days, so tomorrow will be the day as was planned," she reported.

"Excellent. Let's run through the plan one more time tonight and go for a run again in the morning. We can then relax until we are ready to go."

"Sounds good."

They reviewed the plan in detail, and Alan felt good about Lynn; she was ready.

They took their morning run and relaxed and rested all day, preparing for gearing up at 8:00 p.m. and pushing off at 10:00 p.m.

At 8:00 p.m. Alan came out of his room fully geared up for the mission. He was dressed in black cotton pants, a black long-sleeved T-shirt, black socks, and running shoes. He was also wearing a black combat vest that held a head-mount mono night-vision scope and four magazines for his Beretta 92S pistol. His black leather shoulder holster was under his right arm with his Beretta and silencer. He had an additional black shoulder holster under his left arm with an automatic three-shot tranquilizer gun designed and used exclusively by the CIA. The darts contained an extremely strong induced-coma drug that could take down a rhino. He also had his combat knife in a sheath on his belt. He laid his black Gore-Tex rain jacket on the sofa and waited for Lynn to come out.

Lynn came out of her room also fully geared in the same manner as Alan. They checked each other's gear, including their black field packs, and all was found in good order. Alan made green tea, and they sat at the dining-room table.

"You ready for this?" Alan asked.

"You bet. I have run through the details all afternoon, and I am ready," Lynn quickly responded.

They spent the next hour and a half going over all the details of the mission one last time, with Alan answering the few questions Lynn had from her review during the day.

At 10:00 p.m. they got in the black Mercedes AMG sedan, with Lynn driving. They drove to the park next to the grounds of the Grand Hotel and parked on the street near where the western tunnel doors were located. The tunnel was built in the fifties as a bomb shelter due to the threat from China. The tunnel was 180 meters long and led up to the basement in the hotel. The tunnel had been closed to tourists due to construction repairs. They moved to the tunnel-door location, avoiding the one camera that covered the front of the door. Lynn found the hidden door and key pad and pulled the camera display-loop device out of her pack and carefully, working from the side, installed the device on the camera.

The device would record the next five minutes and then continue to loop back the same five-minute recording until removed. They now would be able to exit out in an emergency without being recorded by the camera.

They waited five minutes and then used the pad code that had been provided by the backroom logistics guys to open the door and turn off the alarm. They slipped on their mono night-vision gear before entering the tunnel, which had minimum lighting. The mono scopes worked perfectly, as their eyes automatically shifted to the eye with the night gear, giving perfect vision in the tunnel. By the time they had traveled fifty meters, they had completely adjusted to the mono night-vision gear. They reached the top of the stairs at the door into the hotel basement and used the second key-pad code to carefully and slowly open the door.

As per the intel, no one was in this basement area. Lighting was dim, as only a small number of lights were on in the large storage room. Lynn leaned in and again installed the camera display-loop device, and they waited five minutes before entering the storage area. They waited in the storage area until 1:00 a.m., before they moved to the stairwell that led from the basement up to the hotel. There were no cameras in the stairwell or the hotel-floor hallways. They began to climb the stairs to the tenth floor, where both the North Korean rooms were located. They waited in the stairwell door on the tenth floor until 1:30 a.m., before they moved to the North Koreans' two rooms, which were next door to each other.

Alan held his arm straight up and lowered it. The both drew their tranquilizer guns and opened their assigned door and moved into the pitch-black rooms in a low crouch.

Alan moved to where he could get a great shot, covering all sides of the bed. He leaned over and pushed the desk chair into the desk, making a loud noise. The North Korean pulled his pistol with a silencer from under his pillow and sat up. Alan, still crouched down, hit him in both arms and the shoulder, before he ducked back down. The North Korean said something in Korean and tried to get out of the bed. He barely stood up, before he collapsed to his knees, unable to lift his arms, and dropped his pistol to the floor before falling face first to the rug.

Alan closed and grabbed the North Korean's head and violently twisted it, breaking his neck. Alan confirmed no pulse, and at the exact moment, he heard a bang, as if someone had been thrown against the wall from the North Korean's room next door. He pulled his Beretta—the silencer was attached and a round already racked in the chamber—and sprinted for the door. When Alan reached the door, he saw the North Korean down the hall running for the emergency stairwell. Alan ducked in the other room and tripped on Lynn, who was lying on the floor. Alan quickly checked her pulse and saw she was breathing. He took off down the hallway to the stairwell on a full run.

Alan called on his headset to the cleaner. "One NK KIAed, room one oh three two, and Agent Two down in room one oh three four and needs assistance. In foot pursuit of second NK, west stairwell. Over." When he reached the stairwell door, he crouched and carefully opened the door. He could hear the North Korean running down the stairs barefoot. Alan sprinted in the door and began to run down the stairs three steps at a time on a full run. He estimated the North Korean was several floors below him and was moving extremely fast.

When Alan reached the ground floor, he proceeded carefully down the last flight of stairs to the basement, assuring the North Korean was not waiting to ambush. The basement was clear, and Alan ran over to the west tunnel door and immediately jumped into the emergency slide in the tunnel that ran next to the staircase. He could hear the bare feet of the North Korean slapping on the stairs as he ran down below him. Alan was closing.

Alan slid to the end of the slide, ready to fire with his Beretta at any time. He could see the door out was closed, and he sprinted over to the door, crouched, and slowly opened the door. He could see the Korean running approximately fifty yards away. Alan took off after him in a full sprint. The North Korean was fast, but Alan had a longer stride and was closing with his Beretta ready. Suddenly the North Korean heard Alan behind him and slowed to glance over his shoulder. He started to turn and aim his silenced pistol. Alan immediately dropped to one knee and squared the red dot sight in the center torso of the North Korean and fired three quick shots. The North Korean dropped on the spot. Alan jogged over and put one more round in his head. The rounds to the chest had been in a tight pattern. He dragged the body to nearby underbrush and jogged back to the tunnel door and climbed the stairs back to the tenth floor. He was winded now.

Alan knocked with the code on the door of the room Lynn had been. The cleaner opened the door, and Lynn was sitting on the bed and looked okay.

The cleaner was six foot two and weighed in at 210. He had longer dark hair and a beard and was in his thirties. "Got the guy next door in a laundry cart in the other room. Where is the other guy?"

"He is in the park on a direct line seventy-five yards out of the tunnel door hidden in underbrush on the left side of the trail. Put four rounds in him, so there is blood."

"No problem; I will take care of him. She looks fine. Take care," the cleaner said as he left.

"Lynn, are you okay?"

"Yes, except for my ego. That guy was just too quick for me. I missed him with all three darts. When I made the wake-up noise, he jumped out of bed on the side away from me. Tried to take him hand to hand, and he knocked me out," Lynn said quietly, rubbing her head. "He didn't shoot me when I was out. Why?"

"He wanted to leave some room in case he got caught. Killing you would have been a game changer if he was caught. Okay, let's get out of here."

They returned down the stairwell to the basement and quickly slipped off the video-loop device before closing the door. Again, they were completely clean. They did the same at the door out the tunnel and headed back to the parked car, with their Gore-Tex jackets zipped up to cover their gear.

On the trip back to the safe house, Lynn drove and was completely quiet. Alan knew she was running all the different outcomes in her head; so many of them could have ended very badly for her. Alan broke the silence after a half hour.

"Lynn, he was really good; one of the best I have seen. He was super quick. He was taking the stairs down from the tenth floor three to five at a time at a full run barefoot. Don't beat yourself up."

"I have never lost like that…"

"Yeah, but you are still alive to talk about it. Every mission I learn something new. You just did. Always overestimate a one-on-one situation; be well prepared for the worst," Alan finished as they reached the safe house. Alan checked the time at Langley and called Will, who picked up after several rings.

"Will, it went off clean."

"Excellent. The general arrives tomorrow. We, of course, will continue to maintain the extra security measures as well."

"The North Koreans were very good, as we suspected. I would like to fly back through London and spend some time with Natalie after we finish in Hong Kong. Any issues?"

"No, no issues. How long?"

"I will plan on a week after Hong Kong."

"Great, enjoy and give my best to Natalie," Will said before signing off. Lynn arranged for them to fly to Hong Kong. The refrigerator had steaks, and there was a great bottle of Cabernet from California. Alan barbecued steaks and opened the bottle of wine. Lynn was quiet as they ate dinner.

"I hope my performance doesn't hurt my career," she finally said.

"Lynn, only if you had been KIAed would your career have been hurt." Alan chuckled. He got a smile out of Lynn. "Okay, let's do a root cause of what went wrong. It sounds like you set your position and didn't have full coverage of both sides of the bed."

"Yes, you are absolutely right."

"Then, you made your wake-up noise on the side you covered but away from the side you didn't have covered."

"Yes."

"If I had been in that bed, I would have rolled to the side away from the noise, as the North Korean did. If you are set to cover all sides, expect a rollaway from the sound. Okay, write up that mistake in your report. You have now learned a lesson you will never forget. Have the ability to cover all sides whenever possible. Case closed. You are an excellent agent, and I would work with you any time, any place. Let's go take care of this North Korean colonel."

"Thank you. That means so much to me."

They finished dinner and turned in, ready to fly out the next day.

Lynn fixed eggs and bacon for breakfast, before they left for the airport. They flew together to Hong Kong.

# CHAPTER 15

# HONG KONG HONEY TRAP

They landed midday at Hong Kong International Airport. With numerous skyscrapers and mountains located to the north and its only runway jutting out into Victoria Harbor, landings at the airport were dramatic to experience and technically demanding for pilots.

They took a cab to the Shangri-La Hotel, located on the edge of the Central and Wan Chai districts. The hotel was world famous for luxury and service. They checked in under their aliases, and the bellhop delivered their bags to their room on the eighth floor. The room was a minisuite, with a sitting room and a bedroom.

"I will take the sofa," Alan immediately volunteered.

"You are the boss. You should have the bedroom."

"But I am also a Southern gentleman. Ladies get the beds," Alan said with a chuckle and got a chuckle out of Lynn as well.

"Okay, let's review our game plan. I will spend the day tomorrow at the conference to solidify our cover. You go shopping and play the spoiled wife. The North Korean colonel arrives tomorrow, and our surveillance team will pick him up at the airport and follow him to Langham Hotel, in the Tsimshatsul district, where he is staying. Do you know where that is?"

"Sure, it is at Eight Peking Road. I have stayed there before and knew my way around before I studied the intel."

"Excellent. The intel indicates the colonel will be meeting with a Chinese agent tomorrow afternoon. They will have dinner together as well. The colonel's spy business is done after the dinner, and he will start partying—the real reason he comes to Hong Kong. He will typically go to his favorite backroom card game that night. I am set up to play, so this will be interesting," Alan said with a smile.

"I would like to be a fly on the wall."

"The next day he will call the escort service. He likes to spend the day and night with the escort, including taking her shopping and generally playing big man. Given his colonel's salary of USD five thousand, I can only guess his source of money, but intel indicates these trips are fully paid by the Chinese. I plan to take as much as I can at the card game. You, of course, will be the girl sent by the escort service. The protocol is simple. First opportunity you have in the room, stick him with the small plunger injector. Bottom of foot is best, so it is hard to find in the autopsy. But anywhere that allows you to stay safe." Alan paused and leaned back in the chair.

"So how long before he has the heart attack?"

"The planning guys say it happens in five minutes or less, depending on his current health and heart condition. He will feel distress in twenty seconds, so that is your real time to defend. After that he will be struggling and steadily declining until death. No cleaner, this job. Just leave him."

"Is this fake tattoo I am supposed to apply a joke?"

"No. We want to send a clear message to the North Koreans. Apply it on his shoulder. Either one will do," he responded with a chuckle.

"So 'Semper fi' means always faithful?"

"Yeah. It is the US Marine motto. I would love to be a fly on the wall when they get his body back," he said, not able to prevent laughing. "This guy is the mastermind coming after the marine general; karma is a bitch."

"And you want a photo."

"Yeah, it is for the file, of course, and a present for the general. We are going to frame it for him, four-by-six-inch size." Alan could not help laughing.

Lynn brought Alan to dinner at Sun Hing Restaurant, famous for dim sum. It was excellent. They had one drink at the hotel, with Lynn telling Alan when they got back to the room about her recruitment into the Company. They then turned in. Alan made a bed up on the sofa, and Lynn took the bedroom.

The next day Alan spent the day at the seminar for offshore oil-field support and made sure he met as many people as possible to reinforce his cover. He did enjoy discussing the big toys, and they had a large exact-scale model of the raised-bow supply/tug he had operated in the Gulf of Mexico oil patch many years ago.

At 5:30 p.m., he returned to the hotel. Before entering the room, he gave the code knock, so Lynn would know it was him. She was not back yet, so Alan took the time to check in with the surveillance team on the North Korean colonel to make sure everything was going as planned. The team reported all was going as scheduled, and Alan should expect the colonel to show up at the card game as expected at approximately 11:00 p.m. or later.

Alan was resting on the sofa, when Lynn gave the code knock before entering the suite. She had several shopping bags and a big smile on her face. "I bought a new dress to wear tomorrow in the day and tomorrow night if it goes that far. Wait here, and I will model them for you. Hope you will sign off on the expenses."

Lynn came out of the bedroom fifteen minutes later and looked stunning. "This is the daytime outfit. I want to make sure I get his attention." She was wearing a very short, tight, black mini-skirt, with a split up the rear of the skirt. She was also wearing a red-and-white stretch tube top. She had her hair in a ponytail that reached her waist.

"Wow. You can bet I will approve that expense. I can assure you that you will have his undivided attention."

"One more—the nighttime dress," she said as she went back to the bedroom. Fifteen minutes later she came out in a tight formfitting sleeveless black metallic minidress.

"Okay—there is no question you will have this guy's undivided attention. He will be putty in your hands. Of course, I will sign off on the expense. You will knock him dead—so to speak..." They both laughed.

They rested and had room service. At 10:00 p.m. Alan took a cab over to the backroom cardhouse. There were four players when he arrived; he was the fifth. They were playing Texas Hold 'em, and the ante was five hundred US dollars a hand. Alan was an excellent poker player—extremely good at bluffing when he needed to. He gave away no "tells," in poker or his black-ops work. After an hour and a half, Alan was up twenty thousand dollars, and one of the players had dropped out.

The North Korean colonel arrived later than expected, and he had been drinking. He sat down and bought ten thousand dollars in chips and began chain-smoking cigarettes. Alan pulled out a Montecristo Cuban cigar to help overcome the cigarette smell and smoke. The North Korean was not a good poker player; that was apparent right away. He had also been drinking too much to play—a rookie mistake never made by smart card players, given the adverse impact on their decision making. In a short time, Alan had won half of the colonel's chips, and the colonel was not happy.

"You are an American?" the colonel finally said, with obvious disdain, in excellent English.

"Yes, I am. I am here for a convention. Are you Korean?"

"Yes, I am. I am from Seoul, and I am a rich businessman. I plan to not only win my money back but also all of yours."

"Good luck."

In the next hour, the colonel lost all the chips he had bought and bought five thousand more, which he lost over the next hour. Alan had over sixty thousand dollars in chips. The colonel was fuming as he stood up and pushed his chair over as he moved away from the table. One of the Chinese security men came over and picked up the chair. The colonel watched Alan play, glaring at him for another thirty minutes, before he stormed out.

Alan cashed in his chips and walked back to the hotel on full alert, knowing he had one highly pissed-off colonel who might try to get his money back any way he could. He used the knock code on the suite door before he entered, and he found the door to Lynn's bedroom was closed.

Good, he thought. She will need the rest for tomorrow.

Alan had a small bottle of wine from the minibar to take the edge off, before he crawled on the sofa and went immediately to sleep.

Alan and Lynn had breakfast, and at 10:30 a.m. the telephone rang. It was the Company team that had rerouted the escort-service telephone line so they would first answer waiting for the colonel to call. They advised Lynn the colonel had ordered an escort to meet him at his hotel room for lunch, shopping, and a late dinner as well as to spend the night.

She was packed up, ready to go, dressed in the miniskirt and tube top, and wearing her hair in a ponytail. She left at 11:30 a.m. to catch a cab over to the colonel's hotel.

She rang the doorbell of the colonel's suite; in a few minutes, he answered the door. "Come on in. You can call me Jim. What is your name?"

"Cinnamon. I am very pleased to meet you. I understand you are a very important client of our company. I am here to make sure you remember this day and night for the rest of your life."

"Those are very high goals, but I am pleased you will try."

"First, I would be honored to provide you my specialty. I am an expert in reflexology for your feet and acupuncture treatments that will make you feel great and give you more energy. Can I do that for you now?"

"That would be most excellent. We can then go shopping, and I will buy you presents, and we will have a five-star lunch."

"Please go and change into a robe, and soak your feet for five minutes in as hot water as you can take. I will set up here and be ready when you come out."

The colonel led her into the bedroom of the suite and went back to the bathroom and closed the door. She could hear him running the water. In five minutes, he came out in a white terry-cloth robe and slippers supplied by the hotel.

"Please lie down and let your feet come to the end of the bed." Cinnamon had already laid out her acupuncture needle kit as well as the wooden stick she would use for reflexology, and she pulled over a chair. She did thirty minutes of reflexology on each foot, and she could see the colonel was completely relaxed and deeply enjoying the treatment.

"Was that good?"

"Absolutely the best I have had. Where did you learn?"

"Bangkok. Okay, now I am going to start the acupuncture. You will occasionally feel a small amount of pain when I hit an area where you are having problems in your health. It may hurt for a second. I will write up a report on my findings when I am done."

"This is simply amazing."

She placed the first several acupuncture needles, and the colonel didn't feel them. She picked up the injector and plunged it in in between his big toe and the next toe. The colonel jumped and lifted his foot.

"That hurt!"

"I am so sorry. For your information, that was an acupuncture point tied to your heart. Have you had any heart problems?"

"Yes, I have high blood pressure. Are any others going to hurt?"

"Let me work on another area. I can come back and do a light test at the end in the heart area," she responded as she set the bezel on her watch for five minutes.

After two minutes the colonel tried to sit up. "I am not feeling well. I am dizzy and feeling very light-headed!"

"Do you want me to call a doctor?"

"No. I have to leave tomorrow, and I don't want to see a doctor. Let me rest, and I will be okay."

Lynn sat quietly in the chair at the end of the bed. She could see the colonel was having difficulty breathing. Suddenly he moaned, "Call a doctor. I need a doctor..."

Lynn checked her watch, and four minutes had passed. "I will call you a doctor right away," she said as she got up and walked into the sitting room. She heard several more moans, and then it was completely quiet in the bedroom. She carefully looked in around the edge of the door, and the colonel was lying flat, not moving. She quickly checked his pulse; he was gone. She pulled the arm down on his left shoulder and carefully applied the "Semper fi" temporary tattoo and pulled out the very small camera she had in her bag, took several photos, and pulled the robe back up.

In five minutes, she had packed up her gear and was wiping down the room in the few areas where she had touched. There were no cameras on the guest floors, only in the elevators and lobby. As when she arrived, she went down the two floors and caught the elevator. Cabs were waiting outside the hotel, and she went back to her hotel. She made the code knock and entered the suite. Alan was behind the sofa with his Beretta when she came in the door.

"Wow. You scared me."

"Just being careful. You are back so early?"

"He fell for the reflexology and acupuncture immediately, as soon as I arrived. Mission complete. His tattoo was applied, and I have your photo."

"Excellent. I will book us out tomorrow. I am flying to London. Do you want to go back to Taipei?"

"Yes. Let's fly out in the morning. I want to unwind and enjoy myself here in Hong Kong for the night."

Alan called logistics and made their flight reservations for the next morning. They had an early dinner, and Lynn decided she was going to go out. Alan crashed on the sofa with the TV remote control. Lynn changed into her new formfitting sleeveless black metallic minidress and left.

Lynn finally gave the door-code tap at 2:30 a.m. Alan pulled his Beretta and was behind the couch. She sheepishly came in. "I'm home, dad. Good night," she said with a chuckle. It was obvious she had had a few cocktails.

They left together the next morning for the airport. "You have a good time last night?"

"Yes. Got to see an old boyfriend."

"Great. Glad it worked out."

"Thank you so much for working with me. I was honored. I will get my report to you tomorrow," she said as she gave him a quick hug and a peck on the cheek.

Alan ordered a bloody mary after takeoff.

Damn, that was fast and clean, he mused. I have to give kudos to the backroom guys again.

# CHAPTER 16

## ENGLAND—A WISH-LIST CHECKOFF

Natalie was waiting outside Immigration and Customs at Heathrow when he cleared. She was dressed in jeans and a sweater, and her hair was in a ponytail. She looked beautiful.

"Hello, mate. So glad to see you," she said as she hugged him and kissed him deeply.

"Wow, certainly glad to be here."

"I have us all set up. You plan the Bahamas sailing trips, and I plan this side of the pond. Got my car in short-term parking. Let's go."

Natalie's car was a brand-new Platinum Mercedes E Class AMG sedan. "Wow. I see now you are a much higher pay grade than I am."

"No. Family money, I must confess. Speaking of which, we are going to spend a day and night at the family house. I also have another big surprise: a golf outing with my father and brother."

"Wow again. That definitely is a surprise."

"Settle down, mate. I will run over everything after I get you back to my flat and I make you weak from sex," she said with a chuckle.

The drive was forty-five minutes, and Alan explained he had just finished his first assignment in Asia Pacific.

"How was it, not speaking the language or knowing the lay of the land?"

"They gave me a great partner; could not have done it without her."

"Damn. Don't tell me you got another wife," Natalie said, not able to keep from laughing. Natalie had posed as Alan's wife last year on an assignment.

"Damn right. I am starting to worry about future alimony," Alan said, not able to stop laughing.

"Tonight is a night out on the town in London—dinner at my favorite sushi restaurant, with music and dancing after. Want to show you off to my mates."

"Works for me," Alan replied as they pulled into an electronic gate-drive parking area in very high-end area of Chelsea. "Wow, definitely over my pay grade…"

Natalie led Alan into the second-floor flat. It was a beautiful two-bedroom flat, high ceilings with crown molding, and extremely well appointed. "Wow" was all Alan could say.

"Enough talking, mate." Natalie pulled Alan back to the bedroom.

That evening they had an incredible dinner at a local sushi restaurant before heading to a nightclub in Belgravia. It was a great night of dancing, and Alan got to meet Natalie's friends, who were all friendly and fun. Natalie signaled it was time to go at midnight. "I am ready to go home," she said with a sexy smile.

The next morning, they packed up to drive to the Royal St. George Golf Club with a tee time at 10:00 a.m. Natalie explained women were not allowed at the Royal St. George Golf Club, and Alan would be playing with her father, brother, and a business associate of her father. Natalie advised that her father, Sir Richard, and her brother, John, were in the oil-trading business and were quite successful. They were used to winning.

Sir Richard was in his early sixties, a tall, fit, distinguished gentleman with silver-gray hair. John was a solid athletic six footer with dark hair and blue eyes, just like Natalie.

Alan had brought his golf shoes and a golf glove and Titleist golf balls and only needed to rent clubs. The golf course was a classic links course right on the coast. There were wicked six-foot-deep pocket bunkers all over the course. This course was on Alan's bucket list of golf courses he wanted to play. The wind was down, so it played easier than was typical. Alan was provided an excellent caddie. Alan teamed with Sir Richard; John was teamed with Robert, the business associate. Alan played well with a great short game and putted well with some long putts sunk. They had a great match, with Alan and Sir Richard winning two in one. Alan won the match on the seventeenth, a par four, with a ten-foot par putt. They had a drink in the bar. Alan found out the bet had been for five hundred pounds—when they had said a bet of "five," he thought it was five pounds—and was sure glad he had won. They drove back to the house in Sir Richard's Bentley, as Natalie had already driven back.

The house was actually a gated estate with extensive grounds and thirty-four rooms. Natalie introduced Alan to her mom. She was a beautiful woman with the same blue eyes and hair color as Natalie and in very fit shape. She appeared in her midforties, but Alan knew she was definitely older. Natalie led Alan up to his room so he could shower and change. He had just gotten out of the shower and was at the dresser, when he felt someone behind him in the room. He spun and dropped in a crouch.

"Easy, mate." Natalie chuckled, standing in a false door that led into his room. "This was the headmistress's room. I guess that means I am part headmistress back there somewhere."

They both laughed, and Alan went over and grabbed her, pulling her to the bed.

"Down, tiger…I will see you tonight. Now don't attack me tonight when I come in this door to take advantage of you. Mom is keeping it quite proper separating us. Time to go down for tea."

After tea, Natalie took Alan for a tour of the grounds. The grounds were perfectly manicured gardens, approximately three acres, which kept two gardeners hard at work. "Natalie, I have to thank you for your service with us. It is obvious you certainly don't need the work or money."

"Alan, I decided I was going to make a difference. Working for the SAS, I was only reacting. When the Company came to me, it gave me a chance to actively make a difference. I jumped at it."

"I hear you. That is how they sheep-dipped me in 'Nam. But you are originally a Brit?"

"My mom is an American. I know she speaks as if she is a sixth-generation Brit. I have dual citizenship. She thinks you are handsome and dashing, by the way, but somehow have a dangerous edge."

"She thinks I am handsome and dashing?"

They both got a good laugh out of that.

They rest of the day was fun learning about Natalie while she was growing up. Alan's cover was as a marine consultant, and he discussed some of the projects he had completed. Dinner that night was a formal setting. They ate an excellent rack of lamb and drank several fifteen-year-old bottles of French Bordeaux. Alan had a great time with an amazing family. Alan had a cognac in the library with Sir Richard, John, and Natalie, before they went to their separate rooms. A half hour after they both had retired to their rooms, Natalie showed up in his room through the hidden door.

The next day Natalie and Alan left to fly over to Paris to catch the train to Bordeaux. They checked into the Grand Hotel, using their husband-and-wife covers from last year. They spent their time in the spa, wine tasting in the countryside and enjoying the excellent gourmet food at the hotel restaurants. Alan bought Sir Richard a five-hundred-pound bottle of Bordeaux with his golf winnings as a thank-you gift. They had an excellent time and were extremely comfortable together. Natalie insisted on paying for the hotel, as Alan had paid for the sailing trip.

They flew back to London, and Natalie waited at the gate for Alan to board his flight back to Miami. "Well, mate, outstanding time with you, as normal," Natalie said with a big hug and kiss. "Dad thinks you're quite something, especially winning at golf. As you know, Mom thinks you are dashing and handsome but have a dangerous look; little does she know…"

"They were great. Thank them so much for hosting me. The golf was outstanding. I will, of course, write a note as well as send your mom flowers."

"Oh wow. She is going to really like that. Take care and talk soon," she said as she gave him a last big hug and a deep, long kiss.

# CHAPTER 17

## A ROCK STAR AND STRANGE NEW INTEL

Alan called Will from the dock pay telephone as soon as he got back to the *Anne Bonny*.

"Will, I am back and wanted to check in. Any word on the leak?"

"No. The top guy is about to blow a gasket. He has now set up his two top aides for lie-detector tests. This is never done; normally they just do their typical annual test. We have turned this place upside down, and we are really reaching the end of the rope. I will let you know once we have anything."

"Wow. This is simply hard to believe."

"We all agree. Also got some more bad news. Ed had replaced the key officers and sergeant major and the other positions of the Second Battalion, but apparently the drug smuggling is continuing. We are getting reports from the Costa Rica federal police that the drug smuggling stopped after you eliminated the bad apples. Now the drug smuggling is back stronger than before. The good news is there have been no reported war crimes; the villagers are fine, and the Contras are now delivering medical supplies as they were supposed to have been doing in the past."

"What the hell? How is that possible that there is drug smuggling again? Ed said he had some top candidates for replacing the commander, XO, and sergeant major. This makes no sense they would turn around and immediately be corrupted."

"Ed is heading back out tomorrow to see if he can determine what is going on. He has a few trusted troopers from whom he should be able to find out something. I will let you know once Ed gets back with his report. This is all a real puzzle. The whole thing is really squirrelly."

"Yes, please let me know. I am at a loss to figure this out."

Alan spent the rest of the day cleaning and preparing the *Anne Bonny* for a five-day charter. He was sailing a famous rock-band singer/drummer and his girlfriend out to the Cat Cay Yacht Club and then anchoring and waiting to sail them back after they stayed two days at the club. The charter fee was five thousand, so Alan welcomed the work.

The guests arrived the next morning by a stretch limo with great fanfare and way too much luggage, all in hard-case suitcases rather than duffels. Alan figured out a way to store the empty suitcases in his cabin, and they were under way shortly. The rock star went below and opened a bottle of champagne, and he and his girlfriend began to drink. His girlfriend went down below and came out in the smallest string bikini Alan had ever seen. She laid out a towel, sunbathed, and drank champagne.

The rock star kept asking Alan if he wanted a drink; Alan kept telling him no each time. Once they had cleared the ship channel, Alan asked if they wanted to take the helm. The rock star wasn't interested, but his girlfriend immediately came over and asked to learn to steer the yacht. She caught on quickly and was really enjoying sailing the yacht. She also decided she would openly flirt with Alan while he sat keeping an eye on her at the helm.

The rock star started fuming and began to yell and berate her. They proceeded to get into a shouting match, before the girlfriend stormed down below. It was obvious they had arrived drunk; now they were even drunker after the bottle of champagne. This, of course, was Alan's worst nightmare for charters. They both finally went below, and all was quiet for five hours.

They finally came back from below and appeared to have napped and sobered up. Fortunately, the rest of the charter went well. Alan received a fifteen-hundred-dollar tip, a signed record album, and an apology from both before they left the yacht. The girlfriend also slipped Alan her telephone number. All's well that ends well, he thought. He threw away the girlfriend's telephone number as soon as he went below.

Alan was washing down the deck when his pager went off. He walked to the dock pay telephone.

"Will, you paged?"

"Yes, Alan. I have some really bad news. Ed was ambushed and killed on the way to visit the Second Battalion. This happened yesterday. I knew you were tied up on the charter and didn't want to bother you when there was nothing you could do."

"Fuck! How could that happen?"

"We don't know, but we are sending Wild Bill, given his knowledge of the lay of the land, with three other operatives, to find out what happened. The Contras are telling us they have no idea who ambushed Ed; they discovered his body in his vehicle. This, of course, rings hollow, but we still don't have any idea how this happened. Ed's previous report was excellent regarding the Second Battalion operations, and he had no idea they were still smuggling drugs, until we heard from the Costa Ricans."

"Damn, Will—call that team back. You have no idea what happened to Ed. I believe you are sending these guys into another ambush. We need to know more before we take any action on the ground."

"The top guy wanted someone in as soon as possible there on the ground."

"Tell the top fucking guy I want those guys pulled. I will go back and lead an investigation and assure him I will resolve any issues on the ground there. Those guys are in grave danger. I don't care how good they are; they are walking into an ambush."

"Okay, I will go to the top guy and let him know your concerns. I will get back to you as soon as I can."

Alan went back and sat just stunned in the cockpit. What the hell was going on down there? He was totally lost and had not a single reasonable assumption on how this had all occurred. It made no sense. Damn, he thought. Can't believe they sent Wild Bill and his team in without proper intel…

Alan's pager went off, and he ran down to the pay telephone and called Will.

"Just finished with the top guy. We sent a page message to Wild Bill and his team to immediately withdraw and return—urgent danger. The top guy wants you to take charge of the investigation and the final resolution down there. I will page you back as soon as we know they are out."

Alan went back and again sat in the cockpit to wait. Wild Bill was really good, but some bad shit was going on down there. Ed was a top asset, and they still had gotten him. Alan sat quickly running all the details through his head, trying to figure how this all fit together and what was going on. Waiting was always the hardest part. Alan turned in for the night, pager next to his bed, with no word on Bill and his team. He woke up several times with dreams of Wild Bill and his team being ambushed.

At 6:00 a.m., he called Will from the pay telephone. "Will, what is the word?"

"Nothing. We didn't get the acknowledgment code back yesterday. We haven't heard anything since we sent the withdrawal—urgent danger code."

"Oh fuck. Damn, Will. You know protocol is to respond immediately. Something is wrong. Contact the Costa Ricans and have Special Forces teams go up and scout the area south of the Contra base at Bill's new planned encampment. I want to fly up to Langley

today. Son of a bitch. You sent those guys into a trap without proper intel. What the fuck, Will."

"Alan, calm down. I know; you don't have to tell me. Both the
top guy and I are taking full responsibility for this mistake. I still
hope Bill and his team are okay, maybe just being held captive. I
was just going to tell you that the top guy wants you to fly up. You
won't believe it. His top assistant, Bob, whom you met last year
when you hitched a ride to London with the director, failed his
lie-detector test. We are all in complete shock. I will give you a full
brief when you arrive. You won't believe this shit."

"Will, be realistic. The Contras would never hold those guys
captive. That would assure we knew they were the problem. I will
see you as soon as I land. Have logistics have a ticket waiting for me
at the Miami Airport."

Alan threw some clothes in his bag, locked up the *Anne Bonny*,
and jumped into a taxi to the airport. The first-class ticket was
waiting for him at the counter, and the car was waiting at Dulles
Airport to take him to Langley. He went straight up to Will's office. It was 7:00 p.m., but the light in Will's office was on, and
Alan walked right in. He was surprised to see Eric, the top guy for
operations.

"Alan, we have been waiting for you," Eric began. "I want to
first say I was wrong to have sent Bill and his team without sufficient intel. This is my responsibility, not Will's. I want to get that
off the table."

"Sir, I understand."

"I sometimes think you guys can handle anything. Okay, Will,
give Alan a brief of what we know."

"As I mentioned, Bob, Eric's top assistant, failed his lie-detector
test. He is dating Colonel West's secretary. No shit. You can't make
this stuff up. So she is having dinner at his apartment, and now we
have found out they talked shop on a regular basis. He tells her,
apparently to impress her, that *he* is running a special operation

down south, near where her Contras in Costa Rica are operating. He had sent four top-notch operatives, and they were cleaning up a mess down there." Will paused, leaning back to await Alan's reaction.

"That motherfucker. Are you telling me the secretary then went back and told West, and he alerted the Contras to come after us?"

There was dead quiet in the room. No one spoke for a full two minutes.

"As of now we don't have any other explanation, as crazy as it sounds. Even crazier, West is also sleeping with his secretary. We put him under surveillance after Bob's failed lie-detector test."

"This is batshit crazy. Get West in for a lie detector."

"Well, Alan, here is where it gets really complicated. We need to know who, if anyone, West reports to who knows what is going on with the drug smuggling and now the death of a CIA operative. We don't want to let West know yet what we know."

"What about Bob going right back and telling West's secretary he failed the test, and we know?"

"That won't happen. Bob is under threat of lifetime jail right now, and he is cooperating completely," Eric said with disgust.

"We have the Costa Rican Special Forces searching the area where Bill and his team were set to camp before they started operations. Eric is providing you two dedicated top backroom guys for you to work with on this mission moving forward," Will said as he turned to Eric.

"Alan, your assignment is to search and rescue Bill and his team as well as complete a full investigation of the Contras, the drug smuggling, and the murder of Ed. You will have unlimited access to intel and unlimited resources. We have set you up an operations room with the backroom guys downstairs. FYI, we are also elevating you two pay grades to reflect this change in responsibilities in the Company," Eric finished, leaning back, and waited for Alan to respond.

"Roger that, sir. I will go down to the operations room now to monitor and coordinate with the Costa Rican Special Forces search and rescue," Alan said as he got up, shook hands, and left quickly for the operations room.

Eric and Will sat quietly for several minutes. "We are going to have to make sure Alan doesn't decide to go after West," Will finally said.

"I was thinking exactly the same thing," Eric said as he got up and shook hands and left.

# CHAPTER 18

## SEARCH AND RESCUE (S AND R)

In a half hour, the backroom planning guys had brought Alan up to speed on the Costa Rican Special Forces search and rescue for Bill and his Wildcat team. The Costa Rican Special Forces had choppered two twelve-man teams from their elite A Company unit to the approximate area where Bill was planning to set up an encampment. They had sent out scouts in all four directions, with four-man teams fanning out behind them to complete more detailed searches. They had been operating over the last twenty-four hours without picking up any signs of Bill and his team, when Alan joined the operations center.

The captain in charge on the ground believed that if Bill and his team received the "withdraw and danger" page signal, they would have withdrawn directly to where they had parked and camouflaged their Jeep, so he concentrated two teams in that direction. The captain had a satellite telephone and was giving reports on a two-hour basis.

The operations line rang before the two-hour time, and the call was put on speaker. "This is Tiger One. We have found three Wildcat team members KIAed ten klicks east-southeast of the expected encampment. We have matched photos, and it is the three team members—not the team leader. Over."

"What is the cause of KIAs? Over," Alan immediately replied.

"Multiple gunshot wounds. We have also noted a blood trail from the location, and we have two scouts tracking. Over."

"Roger that. Continue to keep us closely advised. Over."

"Roger that. Over and out," the Special Forces captain said as he signed off.

Alan immediately called Will. "Will, we just got a satellite call report from the CR Special Forces captain on the ground. Three team members are KIAed. Multiple gunshots. Wild Bill is still missing, and S and R is still active," Alan said with great sadness.

"Son of a bitch. Was this the Contras?"

"We don't know yet. The CR Special Forces haven't seen any Contras in the area. A CR team is following a blood trail from the kill area that they suspect is Wild Bill. I will keep you advised."

Alan waited in the operations room all night, getting update calls every two hours with no new information. He was sleeping on the floor of the small conference room at 7:30 a.m., when one of the backroom guys came in and leaned over to wake Alan. He touched Alan's arm, and Alan was up in a crouch, ready to fight.

"Easy, sir. Good news. We have the CR captain on the line, and they have found the team leader." Alan sprinted out to the operations room. The captain was providing a position coordinates for the medevac chopper pickup.

"Captain, Ghost One. Please reconfirm condition of team leader. Over."

"Team leader has suffered two gunshot wounds—one to the left thigh and one to the right bicep. Both wounds are 'through and through.' He has lost a large amount of blood. We have him under treatment. He is fully conscious and requested I tell Ghost he is okay. Over."

"Do you have your teams set in a defense perimeter? Have you or your team sighted any bad guys? Over."

"We are set in a strong defensive position, awaiting the chopper evacuation. We have an Apache attack chopper on station. Wildcat team leader has much intel on the bad guys. I will have him brief you when we get him back, and he is under care at the hospital. I have basics, but better to wait until he can brief you. Over and out."

Alan jogged to the elevator and went directly up to Will's office. Will had just arrived and had a cup of coffee and was reading overnight intel messages.

"Coffee?" Will asked, and Alan nodded. Will poured him a cup.

"The CR Special Forces team found Wild Bill. He is going to make it. He was wounded but should have full recovery."

"Damn. It is about time we had some fucking good news," Will said as he picked up the phone and called Eric. He provided a summary before he signed off. "Alan, I can't tell you how deeply affected and distressed both Eric and I are with the loss of the three team members."

"I understand. I lost two team members in 'Nam," Alan said with sadness. "Wild Bill will be back to the hospital in an hour. Once they patch him up and make sure he is stable, we will set up a post-action briefing call. CR captain said Bill has a great deal of intel on the bad guys."

"Go get some rest. I would expect we will be conducting future operations, and I have no doubt you will want to be on the ground."

"Roger that. I am going back to the Radisson to take a three-hour nap and shower and change. I will be back here at noon. Please wait for Bill's formal briefing until I get back."

"Roger that."

Alan was back a few minutes before noon and went directly to the operations center.

"Bill is awake and doing fine. He has asked to speak to you only before he completes the general brief," the operations-center coordinator advised.

"Okay. Get him on the line, and transfer the call into the conference room. I will talk with him first and then transfer him out and come out for the briefing."

"Roger that."

Alan grabbed a cup of coffee and closed the door and waited. In a few minutes, the phone rang.

"Ghost, is that you?"

"Yeah, Wild Bill, it's me. How are you feeling?"

"I feel like shit. Those guys are dead because of me."

"Slow down, Wild Bill. Explain to me briefly what happened."

"I made a big mistake. I grouped us in a fire-team echelon to the north. The map I had said we were clear for twenty klicks to the south. I thought if we ran into any patrols, it would be to the north."

"Slow down. Slow down, Wild Bill. Tell me exactly what happened."

"We parked the Jeep in the same place as last time. We headed southeast toward the area we had chosen for the encampment. I should have used the fire-team wedge formation…"

"Wild Bill, those guys are KIAed because you were sent into an extremely dangerous situation without proper intel. The mission was rushed, and you guys didn't have a chance."

"In the middle of the firefight, the pager went off with the withdraw-danger code."

"Tell me exactly what happened."

"We were south and east of our previous encampment, moving in an echelon formation aligned to the north. We were three klicks from our planned encampment when we came to a jungle clearing, and we skirted to the north. I was walking point; I shouldn't have been. I should have been in the fire-team-leader position. We were halfway around the clearing, when we were caught in a massive cross fire from the south. I was about to enter the jungle on the other side of the clearing. They hit me twice, and I fell forward into the jungle. The other guys got cut to pieces. I had to get compression pads on me, as I was bleeding heavily. The team was lying prone at the edge of the clearing, but the bad guys had excellent positions. I had just gotten the last compression pad on, when the firefight went quiet." Bill paused, choked up and upset.

"What happened next?"

"I could see all three team guys were down. I waited a short time, and the bad guys started to cross the clearing toward the downed team members. I had my Stoner Sixty-Three with the one-fifty-round drum magazine. I waited until the eight bad guys were crossing the clearing and emptied the magazine. Got them all; cut all of them in half. Loaded another belt and began to flank to the left around their ambush position. No one else was there." Bill paused to take a drink of water and see if Alan would say anything.

"Go ahead, Bill. Whenever you are ready."

"I went back and searched the pockets for the bad guys in the clearing. The team leader had a map that had been marked up. I found a letter from a girlfriend on one of the other bad guys. The letter was from Colombia. One of the bad guys had dog tags: Colombian Special Forces. Everything has been sent to you by courier," he said as he stopped to take a breath and drink some water. "I knew more bad guys would be coming, so I moved northeast, looking for a good place to lie low. I was losing strength and needed to find a place I could feel safe. Two klicks northeast I found the perfect spot in the jungle high ground. I had excellent views in all directions, plenty of open space around me making it very defensible—an Alamo position. I didn't want to use the pager. It had gone off right when we were under attack. I was worried it was compromised, so I crushed it with my Stoner rifle butt. I saw the CR choppers come in and went and found them."

"Wow, Wild Bill. You did everything one hundred percent right. Don't beat yourself up on your lost team members. You guys should have never been there."

"Thanks, Ghost. I do feel a lot better."

"You guys walked into an ambush. They were waiting to see who would come after Ed. You guys didn't stand a chance. Are you ready to brief the group? FYI, I won't ask any more questions in the brief. I have heard enough."

"Sure, Ghost."

Alan transferred the call out to the operations-center conference-call phone and walked out to the operations center. The entire team was there. Alan asked Wild Bill to brief the team and sat back and listened.

The team spent the next hour listening to and asking Wild Bill questions. Halfway through, Alan's boss, Will, came down from his office upstairs and quietly sat in the corner, carefully listening. When the call ended, Will signaled for Alan to come up to his office.

"Damn. They didn't have a chance. They were given intel that they were clear to the south twenty klicks. We told them the expected threat was the Contras to the north. Alan, I fucked up. This is one hundred percent on me. Eric was not part of the detailed planning. He just wanted someone on the ground ASAP to find out what happened to Ed."

They both sat quietly for several minutes. Alan just didn't know what to say.

Will finally spoke. "Okay. I sent a U-2 reconnaissance aircraft over the area. We are going to find out what is going on before we go back there and resolve this matter. I am turning full operational authority to you from start to finish. You didn't have to review with me. Eric has approved this action. You continue to have unlimited funds, personnel, and equipment as needed to resolve this issue. We want you to stop the drug smuggling, but we also want every one of those fucking smuggling guys down there eliminated. They have now KIAed four operatives on my watch. I want you to rain hell on them."

They both sat quietly again for several minutes.

"Roger that, Will, but I will keep you one hundred percent up to speed once we are ready to make a move. I will be using Rene and Eddie."

"No problem. Unlimited…"

Alan got up to leave but stopped: "What is going on with the leak and Colonel West?"

"Colonel West and his superiors are under full investigation. He has no idea. Now we have the Contras and drug smuggling possibly tied to four KIAed CIA operatives. Eric has advised me you will be kept in the loop, and I will let you know as soon as we know more or plan to take an action on Colonel West and/or others—despite the fact it is way over even your new pay grade. This will take time."

Alan nodded and left to go down to the operations center. The U-2 photos had just arrived. He headed down to the photo-reconnaissance unit.

# CHAPTER 19

## LOCK-AND-LOADING HELL

The two guys handling the U-2 photo analysis were in their twenties and wore with pen pocket protectors. They reported to a wise, experienced fifty-year-old who had worked in this unit for twenty-five years. One of the young analysts nodded to Alan when he walked in. "Hello, sir. We have started our review of the U-2 photos. Will had the aircraft on station for eight hours, so we have a ton of data. Given our initial findings, we believe the U-2 reconnaissance aircraft should make at least one more eight-hour run, two if possible. There is a very large amount of activity spread over a relatively large square-mile area."

"I will order the U-2 up for the next two days. Do you have specific areas for concentration?"

"Sir, if you authorize the flights, we will contact the U-2 operations unit directly to provide specific instructions for the surveillance runs."

"Excellent. And please stop calling me 'sir.' You are making me feel old," Alan said with a chuckle.

"We know your nickname at the CIA is the Legend, but others call you Ghost?"

"Ghost was my call sign in 'Nam."

"Can we call you Ghost?"

"Absolutely. You guys are part of the team. How long before we get the first review?"

"We will work all night and have it to you in the morning."

"Roger that." He left knowing it was in the very capable hands of the backroom planning guys, who would complete an extensive analysis of the photos and provide a detailed report summary.

Alan went in his small office in the operations center and closed the door. He called Rene first. "Rene, have you heard the news?"

"Fuck, yeah. I got notice of the four KIA operators. Ed was one of 'em. I can't believe they got Ed. Son of a bitch. I understand Wild Bill took a couple of rounds and lost the rest of his team. What the hell is going on down there? I can't believe this was done by the Contra unit Ed just rebuilt."

"It wasn't. We are studying U-2 surveillance on an area east-southeast of where we camped. I believe there is a group of bad guys that has taken over the drug smuggling from the Contras after Ed cleaned them up. I will be going after them."

"Fucking sign me up. I will let my boss here at my station know I will be going on assignment. Any details yet?"

"No; the backroom boys are still analyzing and working up options. I just want to assemble the team. I also plan to use Fast Eddie. We also will have anything else we need; no limit on personnel or equipment. Please fly up to Langley as soon as you can. I just sent your boss the authorization."

"Roger that. I will leave this afternoon. See you soon."

Alan called the yacht where Eddie worked next. He gave the captain his telephone number and asked Eddie to give him a call as soon as possible. Fifteen minutes later, Alan's telephone rang.

"Alan, what's up?"

"Eddie, got some real bad news. Ed was KIAed in Costa Rica—ambushed. Wild Bill was sent in and took two rounds. He is okay and recovering well. He lost the other three guys in his team," Alan said, pausing to let this sink in.

Eddie was quiet for a full minute. "Holy shit! Not the fucking Contras. Couldn't have been. Ed handpicked the replacements."

"I can't get into more details now, but I will be leading an action against the bad guys who did all of this, and I wanted you to come."

Eddie didn't hesitate for a second. "Fucking A. I will come. I will do this one for free. Just let me know."

"I will give you twenty-four-hour notice. We will pick you up at the Miami Airport. You will be paid; no arguing on that matter."

"Okay, Ghost; just let me know. Will it be in the next seven days?"

"Yes."

"Roger that. I will let the captain know I have a potential family emergency and will have to leave at any time."

"Roger that. See you soon."

Alan went back to the Radisson to get a good night's sleep.

The next morning, he did his seventy-five push-ups and took a three-mile run. He had been sitting around too much the last couple of days.

When he got back, he called Natalie. He waited a few minutes, before she picked up the line.

"How are you doing, mate? I expect you have been busy. You haven't left me for another of your wives?" she answered with a chuckle.

"I got some really bad stuff going on. Did you see the four ops lost in Central America?"

"Yes, I figured as much. I made sure you were not one of them."

"Well, it is 'rain-hell time.' That is a quote. I am leading the action."

"Can I help? They certainly picked the right guy."

"No, but thank you for your offer. We got it covered. Not that I wouldn't mind having you in arm's reach…"

"No fraternizing with the troops."

"I will see you when this is done. You have to come for a sail."

"You can count on it, mate. Be safe, but rain bloody hell. Call me as soon as you are done."

"That is a promise, mate. This will probably be a few weeks. Take care of yourself."

"Same to you, tiger. Be safe."

At 7:30 a.m. he was sitting at his desk, reviewing the U-2 reconnaissance photos and analysis intel from the previous night. He was stunned by the size and scope of the drug-smuggling operation. The bad guys were doing parachute pallet drops out of a full C-130 belonging to the Colombia air force into a jungle clearing. Alan was shocked. How could that be happening? In addition, the bad guys were moving the drugs to the coast and loading shipments onto fast boats to run up the coast and apparently to rendezvous with ships under way. The photo guys estimated this one airdrop was six tons of most probably cocaine.

Alan leaned back in his chair, trying to guess at the street value of one shipment of six tons of cocaine. He had no idea; he continued to read the report that had a section that addressed estimated values based on the possible type of drugs from Colombia. The six-ton cocaine estimated street value was a hundred million US dollars for this one airdrop. Damn. One airdrop of a hundred million dollars of drugs? How big is this operation?

He spent the next two hours reviewing every detail of the report.

Once we get the next two days of U-2 photos, we should have a good handle, he realized.

He was just walking over to get another cup of coffee, when Rene walked into his office.

"Ghost, good to see you."

"Great to have you on board. You aren't going to believe this shit." They bumped fists, pulling their open hands like an explosion before saluting and hugging briefly.

Rene grabbed a cup of coffee, and Alan gave him the U-2 report. "I got to check with the backroom guys working on assets. Read it and weep."

Over the next two days, Alan and Rene reviewed the U-2 photo reports from the backroom guys. They were delivered to Alan and Rene each morning, and Rene got a good laugh the first time they called Alan Ghost.

Alan reviewed his action plans with Rene. Rene added some excellent ideas, and Alan finalized the plan summary and called up to Will. "Will, we are locked and loaded and ready to go. I would like to give you and Eric a summary before we shove off tomorrow."

"Stand by," he said as he put Alan on hold for a minute. "I will meet you up at Eric's office in thirty minutes."

Alan arrived five minutes early, and Will was sitting in the waiting area. Within minutes, Eric's admin assistant let them know they could go right in.

"Good to see both of you. Alan, I again want to say how distressed I am about the three lost operatives on Bill's team. I understand Bill is doing very well. The buck stops here; I take full responsibility."

"Understood, sir. Wild Bill took several rounds in 'Nam. He is tough as nails."

"Okay. Give Will and me the Cliff Notes version. You were fully cleared to complete the operations with whatever equipment or assets needed without our approval, but I do appreciate the update before you guys shove off."

Alan spent the next thirty minutes providing the overview. They all sat quietly for a minute.

"I understand we have full buy-in by the Costa Ricans. I like this plan. It is excellent and measured to fit the circumstances. You didn't need approval, but for the record, you have my full support. Godspeed."

They shook hands, and Alan went down and told the backroom guys to set everything in motion. He and Rene called Eddie and advised they would pick him up tomorrow at the Miami Airport private-aircraft terminal.

# CHAPTER 20

# RAINING HELL

Alan and Rene left at 7:00 a.m. on a CIA Hawker 700 jet and picked up Eddie right on schedule in Miami. The aircraft was refueled, and they lifted off for Howard Air Force Base in Panama, located on the west coast six miles from Balboa and the Panama Canal Pacific entrance. The Hawker taxied over to the Special Operations hanger.

Alan smiled when he went down the stairway and saw SEAL Commander Welsch and Senior Chief Rundle near the hangar door. Rundle immediately walked over and stood in front of Alan. "Great to see you again, Captain Joubert. Welcome to Panama," Rundle crisply said before saluting.

Alan quickly returned the salute; he could see eight Blackhawk choppers with dual miniguns, two AC-130 Spectre gunships, and three MH-47 dual-rotor choppers parked nearby on the tarmac. Sitting in cradles were three Special Operations Craft (SOC) heavily armed SEAL boats for use near shore and on rivers. The boats were mounted with two miniguns, two light machine guns, and one .50 caliber heavy machine gun.

"Great to see you, Commander and Senior Chief. See, you guys have all your best toys. I want you to meet Rene; he was a sheep-dipped SEAL I served with in 'Nam. Since then we have completed numerous missions together." Alan had also completed two missions in Colombia with Rundle and this SEAL team over the last several years, and they had been outstanding.

Rundle gave Rene a firm handshake and a hug. "Welcome, brother," he said, before he turned back to Alan. "Sir, I am pleased to advise we have almost all the same team members you have worked with in the past."

"Excellent, Senior Chief. Let's meet with your planning team tomorrow at zero seven thirty."

"I will also have the air force major handling the Spooky gunships attending. Has the CR Special Forces commander arrived?"

"Roger that; he has already turned in in his room. He will be in the conference room tomorrow morning," the senior chief responded, before he grabbed Alan and Rene's duffels and led them back to their rooms.

The next morning, they held the planning session and review. The presentation was two hours followed by an hour of questions and clarifications. They were ready to shove off the next night.

After the meeting, Alan and Rene took a tour of the AC-130 Spectre gunships. They were both amazed at how much the aircraft had been developed and improved since 'Nam. They would certainly be able to handle their end of the mission. They also walked over, and Rene gave Alan a walk-through of one of the SOC boats. Rene had used the SOC boats in the Mekong Delta in 'Nam when he was a SEAL. Alan just smiled when they were finished.

The next day Alan spent some time with the Costa Rican Special Forces commander. He was a graduate of the US Officer Candidate School, completed ranger training, and was certified for parachute. He was a real bright guy who spoke perfect English and was ready to eliminate this scourge in his country. Midday his troopers arrived by truck with all their gear. The ground crews began to load ammo after lunch on the two AC-130 Spectre gunships and the eight chopper dual miniguns and were finished by 4:00 p.m.

They all geared up at 9:00 p.m., doing their gear checks on one another in the main hangar. Alan, Rene, and Eddie were geared out in SEAL combat dress, helmets, radio sets, and night vision. The Costa Rican Special Forces were given the same radio headsets. Alan had his folding-stock M-14, Rene had an M16, and Eddie had a Remington M-40 sniper rifle. The Costa Rican Special Forces were dressed out in their signature tiger-stripe jungle combat gear.

Alan held a final brief at 11:30 p.m.in the hangar with all personnel grouped in a circle around him.

"Gentlemen, and I use that term loosely"—which got many chuckles—"we have already briefed all of you on the overview and your roles for this mission. Senior Chief, you were probably surprised this is not a 'kill' mission." This got a laugh from all the SEALs. "We will turn over all prisoners to the Costa Ricans. Not surprisingly, we expect few, if any, prisoners at the drop-and-warehouse area after the Spookies are finished." He nodded at the air force major in command of the two AC-130 Spectre gunships and got a return nod. "Those were the guys who took out our guys. Not looking for any prisoners after at that location."

"This sounds more familiar, Captain Joubert," Senior Chief Rundle quickly responded and got a laugh from the SEALs and, this time, from the Costa Rican Special Forces.

"Okay, guys, let's get this done," Alan finished as he pulled on his helmet. The senior chief and the Costa Rican commander moved their teams out to the flight line. The SEALS would be flying out in the three MH-47 dual-rotor choppers with the three SOC boats picked up by their slings as they hovered above them. The Costa Ricans were flying out in the eight Blackhawks. The AC-130 Spectre gunships were scheduled to take off a half hour later due to their higher airspeed.

The MH-47 choppers hovered three miles offshore from the river mouth, setting the SOC boats in the water to allow Alan, Rene, Eddie, and the SEALS to rope down into the boats. They disconnected the slings, and the boats were started up, ready to go. The SOC crew installed the two miniguns, the two light machine guns, and the .50 caliber machine gun, and the boats were under way.

"Viper One and Spooky One, we have splashed, and we are under way. Ghost One over," Alan advised the Costa Rican commander in the lead Blackhawk and the air force major in the lead AC-130 gunship.

"Roger that, Ghost One. We are on schedule, thirty minutes out from rope down. Viper One over," the Costa Rican commander quickly responded.

"Roger that. We have a go. I repeat, we have a go. Please confirm. Ghost One over and out," Alan replied.

"Roger that. Repeat, we have a go. Viper One over and out," the Costa Rican commander replied.

"Roger that, Ghost One and Viper One. Repeat—we have a go. Spooky One over and out," the air force major responded.

The SOC boats were able to travel at forty-five knots, thirty-five in open water. In fifteen minutes, the three SOC boats entered the river mouth, knowing they were fifteen minutes from the smugglers' dock. As the SOC boats turned the last river bend, they picked up the red low lighting at the smugglers' dock area. As the SOC boats approached the dock area, two sentries opened fire on the lead SOC boat with their AK-47s. The portside minigun on SOC boat one opened fire. A steady stream of light arced out toward the two sentries, and they literally evaporated in the stream of rounds.

Two more men came running down the dock, waving their arms with their hands in the air. Approximately ten more men came out of the nearby building with their hands held high.

The boats came alongside the dock, and Alan, Rene, Eddie, and all the SEALS discharged and spread out. Some teams provided cover at the dock, and the other teams with Alan, Rene, and Eddie moved to the nearby building. One man came out of the building and took a step forward, with his hands still held high above his head. "We don't want trouble. We understand we are under arrest. No one here is going to fight you anymore. If you are going to the other location, they will fight you."

Alan stepped forward. "What quantity of drugs do you have at this location?" he asked as three SEALs walked over and searched the men for weapons before securing their arms behind their backs.

The Costa Rican Special Forces who had roped down from the Blackhawks in the jungle east of the dock had set up their defensive perimeter facing the drop-and-warehouse area, and several units were entering the area with four prisoners.

Alan pulled the man who had spoken with him toward the building and was followed by Rene and Eddie. The man was in his fifties and looked like a typical warehouse foreman.

"Tell me about the men at the drop-and-warehouse location," Alan asked once they were in the building. "I won't let anyone know you have told me."

"They are all killers. We are just the guys who ship the drugs. They killed the Americans in the jungle, and they all bragged they were previously Colombian Special Forces hired by the cartel. They will think nothing of killing any of you," he finished with obvious fear in his voice.

"Are these drugs all cocaine? What type of volume are you moving per week?"

"Yes, all cocaine. We are moving two tons a week, sometimes three. Everything for today is gone. The shipments are delivered offshore to ships in transit as well as run up the coast to Honduras, where they are delivered ashore. I don't know how it moves after we drop it there. Are we going to be taken to US or Costa Rican jails?"

"The Costa Ricans will be taking you guys." Alan could see there was a sigh of relief from the man. "You have been very helpful. You or your men won't be harmed, and they will take you to jail. We are going after the other guys."

"Be very careful. They are pure killers."

Alan brought the man out to the Costa Ricans and called over Rene and Eddie. "We will rope down to complete a damage assessment after the Spookies hit the drop-and-warehouse area. We will take two eight-man SEAL teams with us as planned."

Alan called the Blackhawk lead chopper and arranged for their pickup at the planned LZ for the mission. They were off in a half hour, heading for the drop-and-warehouse area. As they approached the area, they could see the AC-130 Spectre's gunships just starting to circle left of the area, one behind the other, preparing for action. Alan used to call their pylon left flying the "dance of death" in 'Nam. Suddenly, massive arcs of light began to flow down from the AC-130s to the drop-and-warehouse area. The amount of fire coming from the two aircraft was massive, lighting up the entire night for several miles. The impacts and explosions on the ground saturated the area that was the size of a football field. The two aircrafts fired until they ran out of ammunition.

Alan, Rene, and Eddie and the SEALS roped down a hundred yards from the target impact area. Just as they started to rope down, a heavy rain began to fall. They formed into fire-team wedges and moved to flank the site from two sides. They began to see white residue all through the surrounding jungle that was cocaine powder that had been blown up and scattered. The rain immediately began to dissolve it. The target area suffered massive damage. The only comparison Alan had seen in the past was completing damage-assessment recon patrols in 'Nam after Arclight B-52 carpet bombings. The area was one large crater after another created by the 105-millimeter howitzers. The AC-130 Spectre's had loaded up extra heavy on 105-millimeter ammo. There were hundreds of small craters created by the 40-millimeter Bofors cannons. There were nothing but small pieces of the metal building left from the warehouse. They found only small pieces of human remains.

They finished with a final sweep of the surrounding one-mile-area circumference around the site, looking for any survivors. None were found. They headed to the planned LZ, and the choppers picked them up right on schedule, and they headed to the Costa Rican Special Forces air base to refuel before returning to Howard Air Force Base in Panama. They picked up the top smuggling guy and his second-in-command from the Costa Ricans and took them back to Panama as well.

They locked the two smugglers in the Howard base brig. Alan held a brief post-action meeting, thanking the SEALs and the fly-boys for their excellent performance on the mission, before they all took off to get some sleep. Alan called Will when he got back to his room. "Will, one hundred percent success. Mission complete. We have two of the smugglers. All their shooters who took out our guys were evaporated by the Spookies."

"Well, couldn't have happened to nicer folks. Glad you 'rained hell,' figuratively and literally. Well done. I will let Eric know. Call me after you have time to question these guys. You have leeway to offer them some deals to get the information. We don't want to use force; we may need them to testify in the future."

"Roger that. Will call you when we have something new."

The next day Eddie flew home. Alan and Rene gave him a fist bump, pulling their hands back like an explosion, crisply saluting, and a giving a quick hug before he boarded the Hawker to fly home. Alan and Rene set up an interrogation room in the Special Ops hangar and started to question the two smuggling leaders from the river port who had been captured. They provided them coffee, and Rene started the questioning, playing the role of the good cop. Alan leaned against the wall with his arms folded, with his best bad-cop look.

After an hour, they had received a great deal of information. These guys wanted to help in any way they could. They just wanted to be able to go to the United States and be given new IDs for their protection. Rene played good cop perfectly, telling them he would recommend their request if they continued to answer all the questions.

The two smugglers made it very clear the bad guys at the drop-and-warehouse site were all enforcers and killers. They would come regularly to their operation to check on them. They made it clear they would kill them all if there were any drug shortages. The smugglers were very happy to learn they wouldn't have to worry about them in the future.

The one area the smuggling guys appeared to be holding back on was whom they reported to for the operation. They did every-thing they could to not answer this line of questioning, claiming ignorance. Both Alan and Rene saw right through this lack of hon-esty. They were bad liars—no lie-detector test needed.

Finally, Alan came forward and told Rene to get up. Alan turned the chair around and sat down in his place—time for the bad cop. "Okay, guys. You have been truthful and very helpful un-til now. You know the person you report to for the operation, and you know where we can find him. You are leaving me no choice. I will have to fly you back to Cartagena and turn you over to the car-tel and tell them you are the reason they lost several hundred mil-lion dollars of their drugs. I don't want to do that, but you aren't giving me any other choice."

The look of abject terror overcame both men. The younger man began to tremble. He was the first to speak. "If we know for sure we will be given asylum in the US and new IDs, I will tell you his name and location."

His boss glared at him but didn't say a word.

"I will guarantee you will be given asylum and new IDs. I can have the base lawyer provide a document with the guarantee."

Finally, the older man spoke. "Get that for both of us, and we will tell you his name and where to find him. After that, we don't have anything else we haven't told you."

"Okay, I will go get the document. We will arrange for lunch to be delivered in here to you. We will be back this afternoon with the document," Alan said as he got up, and then he and Rene left the room. They immediately went next door to the room that provided video and audio from the smugglers' room. The video equipment was hidden in the prisoner room; there was no way they would see they were under surveillance.

"You shouldn't have said we would give them the name and location. We could have gotten by giving less, with less risk to us," the older smuggler said first.

"I just want to be safe and start a new life. I believe the second guy would send us to Cartagena. He knew we had the info. I don't know how, but he knew," the younger man, still visibly shaken, replied.

Alan and Rene came back in the afternoon with the document. Rene provided each man with his separate document—time for good cop again. They carefully read the document. Finally, the older man spoke first. "I am not a lawyer, but this appears to be a plain-language agreement. Thank you for providing it in Spanish. I am ready to talk."

"So am I," the younger man, still very jittery, replied immediately.

"The man who runs the entire money side of the operation we report to is Andre Gomez. He works at a financial company in San Jose, Costa Rica. We don't know the name or address of the company, but we have both seen him and could identify his photo," the older man carefully said. He leaned back, waiting for Rene's response.

"Okay. We will do some investigating and bring back some photos for you to ID. Do you want some coffee?" Rene replied with a smile.

"Yes, that is kind of you," the older man replied as Alan and Rene got up and left.

Alan and Rene immediately borrowed a car and headed over to the Panama CIA station. Alan knew Fred Bendix at the station from past work in Panama. Fred set them up with computer access and a secure phone line. They first called the Costa Rica CIA station to have them independently do a search on Gomez. Rene also began a search on the computer. Alan called Langley and gave them the info on Gomez so they could also do a search.

In a half hour, Fred called from Costa Rica. "I got him. The name was correct, and he works at an investment outfit called Ascende."

"Holy shit. I eliminated a guy at that office in 1980 who had been funding the Contras but started to fund the communist Sandinistas. I actually did the wet work at the office—elevator-shaft accident."

"Very creative. I remember hearing about that one. I am sending you info and a photo of Gomez. Let me know if you need anything else."

"Can you start discreet surveillance? Got to be the best you have. We just eliminated a very big part of his operation, and I don't want to spook him anymore and have him run."

"Roger that. I got just the lady to handle this. Alan, given your new pay grade, I don't need any other approvals," Fred said with a chuckle before signing off.

Alan and Rene printed Gomez's photo, along with four other photos of random persons under surveillance in Costa Rica. They returned to the interrogation room, and both men were napping on the bunks when they came in.

"We want to show you some photos—see if you can ID Gomez," Rene said as he sat at the table and pushed the five photos across the table. Both men got up and came over and sat down. They both carefully and quietly examined the photos. Finally, the older man leaned back and slid a photo across the table to Rene. "That is Gomez—no doubt. I have met him three or four times."

Rene picked up the photo and held it up for Alan. He had picked the photo of Gomez. "Okay, guys, we will be making arrangements to fly you up to the US to get your new IDs, and we will also be giving each one of you ten thousand US dollars," Rene said as he stood up.

"Thank you, thank you," both men said simultaneously.

Alan went next door to the secure room and booked flights for himself and Rene to San Jose, Costa Rica, for the next morning. He called Will. "Will, we are following a lead on the top guy running the entire drug-smuggling operation out of Costa Rica. I have already contacted the station there. Rene and I will fly out tomorrow morning."

"Excellent. Thanks for the update. Look forward for your follow-up report."

# CHAPTER 21

## COSTA RICA

Alan and Rene flew out early the next morning, and a car was waiting at the San Jose Airport to take them to the CIA station. They were brought directly to Fred, the station chief. He offered them coffee—Colombian—and they sat down at his small conference table.

"Well, our operative followed Gomez yesterday from his office to his house. She was surprised there were no security personnel at either location. The house is in the mountains in a very rich area. The house has a high-end security system. Do you guys plan to grab him?"

"Yep, we plan to grab him, and we will need a safe house. No physical interrogation; we may need his testimony. Just good cop and bad cop. We have plenty on him to get what we need from him. Top guys will decide what we do with him when we are done."

"Roger that. We have a safe house near his house. We got a rental car for you guys. There is a perfect area near his house—no houses for several blocks. There is also a stop sign. No one knows for sure why it is there; apparently it is for bike riders who use the cross street. You guys could have a minor rear-end accident and grab him."

"Sounds perfect. Your operative didn't see anything unusual?" Alan asked with surprise.

"No. She expected him to be jumpy and looking in all directions. None of that. She said he was smooth and cool—business as usual."

"Well, that is strange," Rene said, leaning back in his chair.

"Here are your car keys. The rental car is the white Malibu Classic in our back parking lot. Go to our armory-and-supply room, and get whatever you need. Our operative followed him to his office this morning. Let me know, and I can page her to take off once you guys send me your pager code that you are on-site."

"Roger that. Thanks, Fred," Alan said as he and Rene got up and shook hands with Fred and went to the armory-and-supply room to gear up.

Alan had no trouble driving back to the Banco Nacional of Costa Rica building. The Ascende office was on the fifteenth floor. Rene found a parking place near the building parking-garage exit. They had a two-hour wait. Rene jumped out and went down the street and bought Cubano sandwiches and ginger ale. The Cubanos were excellent.

At 5:30 p.m., Gomez pulled out of the garage in his black Mercedes sedan and headed for his house in the mountains. Rene waited a few minutes and began to follow him, staying several cars behind him in the city. When they took the exit off the expressway, they were a mile and a half from the planned grab site. Rene waited to close in on Gomez's car, until they reached the block with the stop sign and no surrounding houses. Not a car was in sight.

Gomez rolled up to the stop sign and made a full stop. Rene ran into the rear of his car at about ten miles per hour, creating significant rear-bumper damage on the Mercedes.

Gomez got out and was holding his arms up in the air, very upset. Alan and Rene both got out of the car, with Rene saying

"Sorry" over and over. They all looked at the damages to the car. Gomez then asked Rene for his driver's license and insurance card. Alan pulled his silenced Beretta from the shoulder holster and held it waist high, pointed at Gomez's stomach. Gomez froze. "I don't have any money. Take my watch and credit cards. I don't want trouble."

Rene moved behind him and secured his arms behind his back with handcuffs. "What is going on? Are you police? Why are you arresting me?" Gomez nervously spoke in a high voice.

"Get in your car in the back seat and shut up," Alan said with authority as he pushed him to the back seat of the car. Alan drove Gomez's car, and Rene followed him to their safe house. Alan parked Gomez's car in the safe-house garage and led Gomez into the back door of the safe house.

"What is going on? I don't understand," Gomez pleaded.

Both Alan and Rene were surprised by how innocent Gomez sounded in the situation. Alan sat Gomez at the dining-room table and pulled up a chair across the table. "If you tell us what we need to know, you won't have a problem," Alan began.

"I haven't anything to hide. Are you Americans? I work for your government."

Alan and Rene gave each other a double-take look. "You expect us to believe that?"

"I can prove it. I take incoming funding and provide it to an arms dealer in Panama who pays the salaries and provides arms and ammunition to the Contras. I have the financial records."

"You know this is drug money. You have been to the smuggling location in Costa Rica."

"Yes. I don't have anything to do with that operation other than to funnel the money to the arms dealer. The times I have been there were to review their books. I am not a drug smuggler; I am a finance guy. I was hired by your government."

Alan and Rene sat quietly for several minutes. Gomez looked from one to the other several times, trying to get a read on what this was about.

"Who do you work for in the US government?" Rene finally said.

"I work through a man who deals directly back to Washington. He is a Panamanian, and I believe he is CIA. His name is Ray Roberts. He, of course, is an American."

"Okay, Mr. Gomez. We are going to hold you here tonight. No harm will come to you. We need the contact information for Roberts. As soon as we find him, we will let you go. Follow me. Do you need to call anyone?" Alan said quietly.

"No, thanks."

Gomez followed him into the safe-house lockup room. It had a bed and a bathroom but was completely secure and unescapable. The door was steel, and the walls were cinder block. The room and the bathroom had no windows. Rene came in and put some food and drinks on the small table. Alan copied down the contact info on Roberts, and they locked the door and left to hunt down Roberts.

Gomez had given them Roberts's address, which was an apartment building in San Jose that had security and a doorman. They arrived and parked, and both Alan and Rene entered the apartment-building front door. A doorman was sitting at a desk reading a newspaper.

"We are here to see Mr. Roberts," Rene said politely.

"Mr. Roberts moved out this morning. The building manager and I were very surprised. A small van came, and two men helped him move his things and load them. They just drove away. I asked if he was coming back, and he told me he wasn't. We were very surprised, as he has six months left on his lease. I asked him what he wanted us to do with his apartment, and he told us to leave it alone and left," the doorman said, still surprised by it all.

"We are friends of Mr. Roberts. Can we see his apartment?"

"I don't see why not. Follow me," the doorman said as he walked from behind the desk to the elevator. The apartment was on the tenth floor, and the doorman opened the door for them. "I came up to check it after he left. The place is empty, just like when we rented it to him."

Alan and Rene looked around and went from room to room. They checked several drawers; they were all empty. "Please, I will get in trouble if you search the apartment. I checked it thoroughly after Mr. Roberts left to make sure he was really gone. There is nothing in this apartment that was not part of the rental."

"Thank you for your help," Alan said as he and Rene left and took the elevator down and got in their car.

"Wow, talk about get out of Dodge quick."

"Who the hell is Roberts? Who does he really work for? He is definitely not CIA. Okay. Let's go back and talk with Gomez and see if we get anything else," Alan said quietly.

They spent several more hours with Gomez. He was cooperating completely. They got nothing else from him; he was a "cut man" from the operation, with his only job handling money. He thought he was helping the US government. They showed him their cover DOD agents' credentials and advised they would let him go, but he was not to tell anyone about their meeting. Alan gave him a number to call to get his car fixed as well as if he heard anything from Roberts.

Alan and Rene went back to the CIA station and met with Fred. Fred had no idea who Roberts was or whom he was working for. They completed a conference call with Eric and Will in Langley. They were baffled as well; they would complete a full investigation on Roberts. Fred would pick up Gomez's financial records of the funding tomorrow and send it to Langley. Alan and Rene decided they would be flying home tomorrow: Fred would search for Roberts and grab him if they found him. Everyone was in agreement. Alan expected Roberts was long gone from Costa Rica.

Alan and Rene then met with CIA operative Robin Edgar; he had taken Ed's place, working with the two Contra battalions operating out of Costa Rica. They questioned Robin on the current status of the Second Battalion. He had no problems with the Second Battalion. They were performing without any problems—absolutely no issues. He had never heard of Roberts.

They caught a flight the next morning out of San Jose to Miami. Rene then connected back to Haiti, and Alan returned to the *Anne Bonny*, glad to finally be back home.

# CHAPTER 22

## R AND R BAHAMAS

Alan let Will know the next day he and Natalie would be going sailing in the Bahamas for five days, but he would have his pager. Will had no problem and would monitor and take care of the mission while Alan was gone.

Natalie flew over on schedule, and Alan picked her up at the airport. She looked outstanding as always. They stopped and had a lunch of stone crabs before heading back to the *Anne Bonny*.

They were under way two hours later, on course to North Andros to anchor before sailing to Cat Cay in the morning. After they anchored, Alan barbecued steaks on the back railing grill, and they had an excellent bottle of Cabernet from California.

They were sitting and chatting in the cockpit, when Natalie finally broke the ice. "Are you okay? This last action appeared to have a big impact on you—not something I normally see."

"This one is a real FUBAR. I can't go into the details, but something is rotten in Denmark, and I don't know what it is."

"I can tell it is weighing on you. Follow me for some special stress-relief therapy," Natalie said as she pulled Alan down to their cabin. Natalie was right; it was just what the doctor ordered:

absolute stress relief. They decided to turn in early and get an early start the next morning.

At 2:00 a.m., Alan awoke to the sound of a boat quietly coming alongside where the boarding ladder was down. He quickly tapped Natalie, and she immediately sat up. Alan held his finger to his lips. He pointed up to the deck. They both listened. Alan could hear the boarding ladder pressing and shifting against the hull as first one person and then a second came up the ladder. Alan pointed up and held up two fingers.

Alan reached over and slid back the panel next to the bunk and quietly and carefully removed two Berettas with silencers. He cautiously and quietly chambered a round in the first one and handed it to Natalie. He chambered a round in the second Beretta as Natalie slid out of bed. She positioned herself in a crouch on the side of the cabin away from the door, with the Beretta aimed at the cabin door. Alan crawled out of the bunk on the same side, away from the door, and pulled back the covers. He placed all the pillows in the bed and pulled up the covers so it looked like two people were in bed. They could hear two persons quietly moving on the deck. The main-cabin hatch was opened, but their cabin door was locked. A professional would easily be able to pick the lock on the cabin door. In a few minutes, they heard someone working to pick the lock. Alan lay down flat next to the bunk on the cabin floor. Natalie stayed in a crouch, pressed against the cabinet in the corner of the cabin away from the door.

They heard the lock click, and there was a one-minute pause. Suddenly the cabin door was thrown open, and two men opened up with automatic weapons, emptying both their magazines into the cabin bunk bedding. Alan heard them both run out of ammo and begin to pull their magazines. Alan was at the corner of the bunk on the floor and leaned around the edge of the bunk and shot both men multiple times in the ankles. They fell forward, and Natalie had a clean shot and put one round in each guy's head.

They both waited, listening for any sound that might indicate anyone else was on board. All was quiet. Alan stepped over the bodies and carefully moved to the main-cabin hatch. He cautiously checked the main deck and then the hard-bottom inflatable tied alongside. There were no others.

"Natalie, all is clear."

She came up to the deck and sat on the edge of the cockpit, the Beretta still ready. "What the fuck was that about, mate?"

Alan could see she was shaken, as she had every right to be. "I don't know, but after the last assignment, I may have an idea. Let's go ashore so I can call Langley."

Alan went back and checked both dead shooters. They had on ski masks and body armor. Alan pulled off both ski masks. They appeared to be Central or South American. They were armed with Heckler and Koch HK43 automatic rifles with silencers. Thank heavens they weren't militarily trained; both had emptied their magazines at the same time.

Alan gave Natalie a shoulder holster and a windbreaker, and he put on his shoulder holster and slipped on a windbreaker. They climbed into Alan's dinghy, and he drove full speed to the dock. There was a pay telephone on the dock, and Alan dialed the emergency Langley number and asked for Will. He waited several minutes, before Will came on the line. Alan gave him a brief of the attack.

"Damn! You stay ashore right now. Find a good defensive position. I am going to send an FBI SWAT team by chopper. No telling how many more are out there. Your code is 'Reddog One'; don't leave cover until you get a confirmation from the FBI guys."

"Roger that. We will be in an area with good cover near the dockmaster's office. You need Fred to go pick up Gomez in Costa Rica and hold him under protective custody as soon as possible. Call Rene and let him know they came after me while I was with Natalie.

I'll call Eddie in the morning, but I think he should be okay. I think they are trying to clean up," he said before signing out.

They waited on full alert for just less than three hours, when Alan picked up the sound of a chopper coming in fast and low. He tapped Natalie and pointed in the direction of the incoming chopper. The chopper was clearly marked FBI. When the chopper reached the dockmaster's office, eight SWAT team members in full gear roped down, and the chopper dropped the ropes and took off to the west.

The eight SWAT team members formed a defensive perimeter and remained quiet for several minutes. Two of the SWAT team members were within fifty feet of Alan and Natalie but didn't spot them, as Alan and Natalie were lying flat behind cover. Finally, the SWAT team leader, feeling the area was secure, called out "Reddog One."

Alan responded with the "Reddog One" and slowly stood up. The two nearby SWAT team members were surprised how close they had been. Alan walked out first to the SWAT team leader, who gave him a strong handshake, before he called Natalie out of cover. Natalie was still wearing only a T-shirt and her panties, so one of the SWAT members pulled a thermal blanket from his pack and gave it to her so she could wrap herself.

They walked with the SWAT team to an open field next to the marina, and the SWAT team leader called in the chopper. They all loaded up and were in the air fifteen minutes later, heading for the Florida coast. The chopper landed on the downtown building where the FBI was located, and the SWAT commander brought Alan and Natalie down to their conference room in the SWAT office and showed Alan the telephone and advised it was a secure line.

Alan immediately called Will. "What the fuck was that all about? Two hired killers with automatic rifles try to murder me and my girlfriend while we are sleeping on my sailboat? How did they fucking find me? This has to be blowback from taking out the cartel drug operation and Contra funding in Costa Rica."

"Is Natalie there with you? She isn't cleared for this discussion."

"Cleared for the fucking discussion? Are you kidding? Two men tried to shoot her to death while she was sleeping on my sailboat. She is a CIA black operator. Fuck the clearances."

"Okay, Alan, calm down. I know how upsetting this must be..."

"Fucking upsetting? You have got to be kidding. You have no idea how upset I am right now. I want to know immediately how they found out about me and my yacht at anchor off North Andros. I have been completely compromised by someone. The shooters looked South American; I would bet this is drug-cartel-and-the-Contra-funding blowback. They had no military experience, thank God. They both emptied their magazines at the same time. If they would have used military procedure, only one would have fired, and the other guy would have had twenty rounds to respond when we opened up."

"Okay, Alan, I hear you. Go to a hotel tonight. I will have the SWAT guys in plain clothes drop you off and stand watch. I want you to fly up tomorrow. Bring Natalie."

"Roger that."

The SWAT guys drove them to the Omni Hotel. Natalie tied the thermal blanket in a wrap, and she looked quite avant-garde and stylish. Alan woke up at 6:00 a.m. and put in a call to the yacht where Fast Eddie worked. He had him call back on the dock pay telephone. Alan confirmed he was okay and gave him a brief of what had happened. Eddie was shocked; he confirmed he would be on full alert until he heard back from Alan.

At 11:30 a.m., Alan and Natalie got up and went clothes shopping. Logistics had booked a 2:30 p.m. flight to Dulles, with the tickets waiting at the airline counter.

# CHAPTER 23

## THE RATS ABANDON SHIP

Alan and Natalie reached Langley late afternoon and went straight to Will's office. He was waiting and led them over to his conference table.

"So pleased to meet you, Natalie; your reputation in the Absolute Resolution program is well known by me and Eric. You aren't cleared to sit in, but Eric and I have made an exception because of what happened on the yacht last night. Thank God you guys are top pros."

"Thanks, Will. What's the word on how they IDed me?"

"We got Bob, Eric's assistant, back under the lie detector, and we discovered more details not picked up the first time. He not only mentioned to Colonel West's secretary that he had sent down four guys to clean up; the secretary asked if they were CIA. Bob told her two were CIA, and two were hired contractors. He then gave your name and Eddie's to her," he said as he leaned back and waited for Alan to respond.

"What the fuck? You have got to be kidding. This guy is talking top-secret information over a dinner?"

"He is now in jail, maximum security. Charges will be filed shortly. I know this is of little consequence..." Will replied with obvious disgust. "His defense is they both had high clearance approval, which, of course, is absurd."

"Okay. This all leads back to Colonel West. What is going on with him, and when is he being taken into custody?"

"You aren't going to like this, but right now they are trying to do a deal with him to get larger fish."

"Wait a fucking second. We have four dead CIA operatives. We also have someone who was facilitating the operation of a major cartel to smuggle drugs into the US to fund his little war. He is going to be offered a deal?"

Will sat quietly for several minutes. Natalie had not said one word; she just sat there in disbelief.

"Alan, this is the way the Justice Department works. They want the people at the very top. Let's head up to Eric's office, as he wants to talk with you. Natalie, I have to ask you to wait here."

"Sure. I have already heard enough crazy shit."

Will and Alan went to Eric's office, and they were led right in. "Thank God you and Natalie are okay. I am shocked this was caused by someone working for me. I can't tell you how distressed I am," Eric began. "I am sure you didn't want to hear the news on Colonel West. He will go to jail. They need his testimony to get to POTUS's chief of staff. Without West's testimony, they got nothing."

"So have the shooters who tried to kill Natalie and me on my yacht been IDed? Are they killers from the drug cartel who now know who I am?"

The silence in the room was deafening. For three minutes, no one said a word.

"Colonel West gave the cartel your name. They found you. The shooters were from the cartel. West panicked and was hoping the cartel would clean up his mess. FYI, the cartel got Gomez down in Costa Rica before Fred could pick him up."

Again, there was silence; everyone was trying to absorb the enormity of the situation.

"I want to visit Colonel West in jail. I deserve to talk to him," Alan finally said quietly.

"He is not in jail yet. He has been relieved of duty, but they want to get his testimony and even testimony before Congress. It will be a while before he goes to jail," Eric answered very carefully.

"So what do I do now that my identity has been compromised to the cartel? I can't live on the *Anne Bonny*, constantly on guard, looking over my shoulder. I can't take charters and risk them to danger."

"We are looking at all possible options to offer you. This happened so suddenly, we haven't had time to come up with options. But I promise we will," Eric said with concern.

"What if I just want to quit? I will certainly consider that option. This is just like Operation Phoenix in 'Nam before I left. A massive combination of a FUBAR and a SNAFU all rolled into one. I have to believe in what I am doing. I am putting my life on the line every day."

The room was dead silent. No one spoke for several minutes.

"Okay. I have had enough for today. I need to go sit down by myself and digest everything. I will be at the Radisson; call me when you have options," Alan said very quietly and got up and walked out. He went down and picked up Natalie, and he left to check into the nearby Radisson.

When they got to the room, Alan just sat quietly on the bed. Natalie sat over in the desk chair, letting him have his space. He sat silently for five minutes, before he looked up. "I have been compromised. That was the cartel that came after us."

"Alan, I just can't believe this is all happening."

"I have to go out and take a very long walk. I need to go over and spend some time alone at the 'Nam Memorial. Do you mind my going by myself for a while?"

"Absolutely not, mate. Go out and clear your head. This is simply overwhelming. I think it will be good for you. Take as much time as you need; I will be here for you," she said as she wrapped herself around Alan and gave him a deep kiss.

Alan left at 7:30 p.m. Natalie was exhausted and showered and crawled into bed.

At 1:00 a.m., Alan did the code knock on the door. Natalie pulled her Beretta anyway and got behind the sofa as Alan came in the room.

"What time is it, mate? I have been asleep the entire time. Do you want to talk?"

"No. I want to crawl in bed and wrap myself around you. That is exactly what I need right now," he said as he pulled her back to bed. They both slept soundly until 7:00 a.m., before Alan stirred first.

"I need breakfast and a run and the gym. How about you, beautiful?"

"Works for me, mate," she said with a smile and crawled out of bed to take a shower. Alan showered after, and they both put on their running clothes and shoes and went down to have breakfast.

"Well, mate, any decisions?"

"Yes. Plan to rechristen the *Anne Bonny*. Her new name will be *Islander*...I think I know exactly what I want to do, but I want to keep an open mind and hear what they have to offer," he said with a chuckle.

"Great to hear you positive and light-hearted, tiger."

After breakfast, they spent an hour in the gym and then took the two-mile run Alan normally took when he stayed there. When they got back, it was 10:00 a.m., and the telephone message light was blinking. Natalie jumped in the shower, while Alan checked the message and then called Will.

"How did you sleep last night?" Will began.

"I took a really long walk and went to the 'Nam Memorial and spent time there. That always helps. Then I went back and slept like a baby with Natalie."

"Great. Well, Eric has really worked hard since you left to come up with as many options as he could for you. He really cares about you, Alan."

"I am looking forward to hearing them. What time do you want me to come in?"

"Right now, if you can make it. Eric and I are free until lunch."

"See you in twenty minutes."

When Alan reached Will's office, he was waiting to take him up to Eric's office. As soon as they arrived, they were brought right in and led over to the conference table. Eric came around his desk and firmly shook hands. "Good to see you smiling, Alan. Have a seat, and let's chat and talk about options."

"Will and I have spent all day yesterday and this morning working on what we can offer you," Eric started, leaning back and trying to get a read on Alan.

He was just getting ready to continue, when his admin assistant stuck her head in the door. "Boss, I know you asked to not be disturbed, but the POTUS chief of staff insisted I interrupt you. He wouldn't take no for an answer."

"Okay, Marilyn, put him through. Gentlemen, stand by," Eric said as he walked over to his desk and picked up his phone and pressed the blinking line. "Eric here."

Alan and Will could hear the caller screaming over the phone from across the room; in fact, it was so loud Eric held the phone away from his ear, and he could still hear. After three minutes, the screaming finally stopped. "Hang on, Roger, and settle down. Let me clear my office, and we can discuss this. Hang on," he said as he put the call on hold.

"Guys, I have a crazy man I have to talk to privately and would appreciate if you could wait for a short time outside."

"Of course, boss," Alan said first as he and Will got up and walked out and closed the door. They waited quietly for fifteen minutes, before Eric called and told his admin assistant to send them back in.

Eric was waiting at the conference table. Alan and Will both sat back down and waited for Eric to continue.

"Well, guys, there has been a major new development. POTUS chief of staff is going batshit crazy. Colonel West apparently slipped and fell in his bathroom last night and is dead."

There was complete silence for several minutes, before Alan finally spoke. "Well, either he had a real accident or the cartel decided to eliminate a loose end."

"I said the same thing to the POTUS Chief of staff. He was totally beyond reason and wanted to know if any of the black-ops operators were in town. I told him yes but told him that the information was on a need-to-know basis. Well, that unglued him even more. He told me I would be hearing shortly that he had 'a need to know' and hung up on me."

They sat quietly for several minutes.

"Wouldn't the cartel have made it big and messy?" Will spoke first.

"No, I don't believe so. I wouldn't believe they would want to openly declare war on the upper echelons of the US government. They wouldn't win that war," Alan said, leaning back and stretching.

"I agree," Eric immediately replied. "Maybe it was just an accident."

Will was carefully examining Alan, who was sitting next to him. He didn't say another word.

"Okay, guys. Let's start over on this after fourteen thirty hours today. Let me deal with this issue, as I know he will be back shortly." He started to stand up but stopped.

"Alan, anything we need to know? I fully expect the FBI is going to complete a full investigation, and you will be tagged as a suspect by the POTUS COS. That will carry a great deal of weight. I am sure this means full interrogation, lie-detector tests as well as examining all available video-camera feeds," he said, carefully watching Alan. Will also continued to study Alan from just feet away.

"No, boss. But let me just say, I'm not unhappy that a man who is responsible for the deaths of four CIA operatives is dead—no."

Eric and Will both looked at each other as Alan and Will got up.

"Okay, Alan. See you guys later today."

Alan and Will went back to Will's office and sat at his conference table. Will sat quietly across from Alan, not saying a word.

"Well, Will, I am going to go back and have lunch with Natalie, unless you need me."

"You better wait here, Alan. I will take you to lunch."

Will drove Alan to a nearby restaurant before they went back to Langley. Will had to catch up on work afterward, and Alan went down to the pistol range to pass time. At 2:20 p.m. Alan was waiting in Eric's office when Will walked in. The assistant brought them right in and led them to the conference table. Eric was waiting at the table.

"Well, guys, the shit has hit the fan. I had to let Roger know you were in town, and he has personally decided you killed Colonel West. He is irrational. He spent the last hour with the director of the FBI. They want to come over and interrogate you now as well as conduct a lie-detector test with their personnel administering the test," Eric said with concern and tapped his pen on the table.

"Fine. I am ready. Let's get this done," Alan said as he stood up. Will led Alan to an empty conference room and left him to wait for the FBI team. Six agents showed up; two were from the lie-detector team. They videoed the interrogation while he was hooked up to the lie detector. The interrogation lasted three hours before they completed the final wrap-up of questions.

"Mr. Joubert, thank you for your time," the special agent said as the lie-detector team packed up. "Also, thank you for your service," the special agent finished before firmly shaking Alan's hand.

Alan went back to Will's office, where he was working at his desk. He looked up with a questioning look. "They are finished for today," Alan said with a smile.

Will could not help smiling back. "Anything Eric and I have to worry about on our end?"

"Nope. I am going back to have dinner with Natalie. What time do you want me here tomorrow?"

"I will send you a page later this evening," Will said as he stood up and firmly shook hands with Alan before he left.

Alan immediately went back to the Radisson and gave the code knock on the door. He was surprised Natalie was not in the room once he entered. In a half hour, Natalie gave the code knock on the door before coming in. Both arms were covered with shopping bags, and she had a big, wondrous smile. "I want you to know, mate, I also went to the Lincoln Memorial as well as the Vietnam Memorial."

Alan went over, and she dropped all the bags and wrapped herself around him and gave him a deep, long kiss. "Need a little stress relief?"

"I am always ready for stress relief," he said as he pulled her to the bed.

They both lay sated an hour later, and Natalie sat up on an elbow and smiled. "Did you hear anything that made sense for you?"

Alan told her the complete story of what had happened, and when he was finished, Natalie crawled on top of him and looked deeply into his eyes. "You pass my test," she said with a wicked smile.

"Well, most excellent. Do you want to eat French tonight? I am sure you have something in one of those bags to wear."

"You bet, mate."

They went for an excellent dinner in Georgetown, and the meal and wine were superb. Alan's pager went off during dinner; Will wanted him in at 9:00 a.m. They had a nightcap at the restaurant bar, before taking a cab back to the hotel to turn in early.

Alan was waiting in Will's office at 8:45 a.m., when he came in. They had coffee and took it up to Eric's office, where they were shown right in.

"Okay, Alan, back to business. I want to review your offers. First, which is part of our first option, is you move your yacht to another location over one hundred miles away. We will have the registration changed, a new paint job on the hull, and you will need a new name," Eric began and paused.

"Excellent. I already have a new christened name: *Islander*. I want to moor her down in the British Virgin Islands."

"Great, we are off to a good start. We also want you to continue your work with the Absolute Resolution program but only operating in Asia Pacific." Eric again paused and leaned back, waiting for Alan to respond.

"Boss, I want my five-year buyout. I am resigning. I will do some contract work but only after I decide it is something I want to do. I will, of course, assure I will continue to handle everything 'top secret.'"

Both Eric and Will sat back; they were surprised and stunned. "Did what occurred yesterday drive your decision?" Eric finally asked after a full minute.

"No. I decided I would leave after this work on the Contra funding was done. I promised myself after Operation Phoenix in 'Nam, I would try to make things right and then walk away. I am done."

The room was dead silent for three minutes. Finally, Eric spoke quietly. "Alan, I want to thank you for your outstanding service for the CIA. The awards issued to you stand as our respect for you. I will arrange for a final settlement of payment of one hundred twenty-five thousand per year for five years, taxes paid. You can keep the yacht. I do want you to maintain your top-secret clearance and consider contract work for Will. You can negotiate your price per assignment. Do you have anything else you want to say?"

Alan stood up. "No, boss. Thank you, and everyone else, for your loyalty and support." Eric and Will stood up and firmly shook Alan's hand and sent him down to the Human Resources office to finalize the paperwork.

Within an hour he was heading back to the hotel. He told Natalie about his decision. She gave him a big hug and a kiss. "I'm jealous." He decided he would spend time in London until his yacht was repaired and transferred to a dock slip in Road Town, Tortola.

# CHAPTER 24

## TWO MONTHS LATER—MEDELLIN, COLOMBIA

It was 1:00 a.m., and Alan and Eddie sat quietly, eating energy bars and drinking water in their perch in the church tower. They were both dressed in black with black running shoes and boonie hats. They had two black ski masks lying close by. Eddie had his custom black L-96 sniper rifle, and Alan had his folding-stock M-14. Alan also had the sniper night-vision spotting scope and took one more look over the edge of the bell-tower wall.

"Isn't it ironic church towers make such good sniper positions?" Eddie quietly whispered and got a chuckle out of Alan.

"The targets should be coming out of the building in the next hour. You locked and loaded?"

"You bet, Ghost. I can't believe we are getting paid fifty thousand tax-free US dollars each for this one mission. You are a hell of a negotiator, Ghost. You know I would have done this one for free for Ed and the other three guys."

"So would I. But I certainly don't mind getting paid fifty thousand to do it—not like we can put 'assassin' on our tax forms. It is really a bonus to have a shot at Roberts, besides the head of the cartel. Roberts was the guy running the drug smuggling. I am sure he was directly related in the ambushes of our guys. Rene and I just missed grabbing him in Costa Rica."

Alan rechecked the target area with the scope; the range was 920– 930 yards. At that moment, three black SUVs pulled up outside the building. Men exited the three SUVs and did a quick sweep of the surrounding street area before the apparent team leader went into the building.

"Here we go, Fast Eddie—show time," Alan said as he handed Eddie his ski mask, and both slipped them on.

Eddie lifted the L-96 sniper over the edge of the clock-tower wall and began to zero in on the center of the target area. Within minutes, a group of men began to exit the building.

"Primary target is second in line. Secondary target is first in line. Primary target is at nine hundred and twenty-eight yards and counting. Minus one, two…"

The silenced L-96 made a coughing sound, and the round left the barrel. Alan focused on the primary target and saw him lunge back and fall—definite spine shot. The secondary target immediately turned and leaned over to check his boss.

"Secondary is nine hundred and twenty-eight yards in a crouch."

"Got him," Eddie responded as the sniper L-96 coughed again. Alan watched as the secondary target fell over the primary target.

"Mission accomplished. Let's pack up and leave. They have absolutely no idea what has happened. Time to get out of Dodge," Alan said as he pulled off his ski mask and began to disassemble his M-14. Eddie did the same for the L-96. They stowed the disassembled rifle components into custom false-bottom fittings in their guitar cases. When they closed the guitar cases and then reopened them, you could see only a guitar in each case. The compartment below could be opened only with a small pin. They locked both cases and slipped on their fedora hats. With their five-day-old beard growth, they looked like a couple of hip musicians.

They quietly walked down the tower staircase. Their safe house was five blocks away, and they were in their separate rooms in bed in an hour—still armed with Berettas under their pillows and on full alert.

The next morning, they drove to Cartagena to fly back to Miami. They made the drop-off of their gear to the CIA operative at the gas-station bathroom near the airport.

They boarded an American Airlines flight, first class, and each had a couple of bloody marys on the flight back. Alan had picked up a copy of *El Tiempo*, the most popular Colombian newspaper, in the airport. The front-page story was about the execution of the top suspected cartel leader. The article speculated it was the work of a rival gang. Alan chuckled and handed the newspaper to Eddie. He took a quick look and just smiled. "Piece of cake." This got a big laugh out of both of them; the flight attendant in the galley briefly looked around the corner to see what was going on. Both Alan and Eddie had big grins, which got one out of her before she ducked back in the galley.

In Miami, Eddie was going back to his job on the megayacht, and Alan was flying down to Road Town, Tortola, to his home on the *Islander*, his rechristened and renamed Swan forty-seven-foot sloop.

Eddie walked Alan to the gate. When boarding started, Alan and Eddie both stood up. They gave each other a fist bump, pulling their open hands back like an explosion, and saluted before a brief hug.

"See you in a week on the *Islander* in Road Town. Natalie is looking forward to meeting your girlfriend. Glad you guys could both come down for a week." Both men smiled before Alan boarded the flight.

Alan ordered one more bloody mary. He planned to nap on the flight down, as it had been a long night. He sat back in the first-class seat and sipped his drink. He had never heard back from the FBI regarding Colonel West. He knew he had passed the lie-detector test, as he had done in the past when he knew he had done the right thing. The West wet work had gone perfectly; West never saw him until it was too late. When Alan had West in a choke hold, he had told him who he was and that it was payback for the four dead CIA operatives.

He was really liking contract work—no strings attached. Five assignments a year would be $250,000. He would be sailing four times a year with Natalie in the BVI and spending five visits a year in London and Europe with Natalie. Most importantly, he got to pick his assignments...

# ABOUT THE AUTHOR

 Al Dugan spent extensive time in Central and South America during his career in the marine-insurance industry.

Dugan grew up in New Orleans, Louisiana. He attended Jesuit High School and graduated from Louisiana State University. Dugan spent thirty-six years in the marine insurance industry including working as an underwriter for Lloyd's of London. Dugan was awarded the Chairman's Award for outstanding service during his career.

Made in the USA
Columbia, SC
21 August 2017